DOCTOR  WHO

Night of the Humans

The DOCTOR WHO series from BBC Books

DOCTOR ⬡ WHO

Night of the Humans

DAVID LLEWELLYN

1 3 5 7 9 10 8 6 4 2

Published in 2011 by BBC Books, an imprint of Ebury Publishing.
A Random House Group Company

The Random House Group Limited Reg. No. 954009

Addresses for companies within the Random House Group can be found at
www.randomhouse.co.uk

A CIP catalogue record for this book is available from the British Library.

ISBN 9781849903110

The Random House Group Limited supports The Forest Stewardship Council
(FSC®), the leading international forest certification organisation. Our books carrying
the FSC label are printed on FSC® certified paper. FSC is the only forest certification
scheme endorsed by the leading environmental organisations, including
Greenpeace. Our paper procurement policy can be found at
www.randomhouse.co.uk/environment

Commissioning editor: Albert DePetrillo
Series consultant: Justin Richards
Project editor: Steve Tribe
Cover design: Lee Binding © Woodlands Books Ltd, 2010
Production: Rebecca Jones

Printed and bound in Great Britain by
CPI Group (UK) Ltd, Croydon, CR0 4YY

To buy books by your favourite authors and register for offers,
visit www.randomhouse.co.uk

For Tim, who listens and makes the coffee

ITEM 8B: Captain's Journal (incomplete/ corrupted)

The following is property of the Intergalactic Environmental Agency (IEA) and may be read by authorised personnel only.

Vessel: IEA BEAGLE XXI (Sittuun Operations, K-Class)

Last known location: Battani 045, Object 556/C - Designated 'The Gyre'

COMM OFF: Cpt. Jamal al-Jehedeh

Report No: 178
Date: 26/11/338ED

At 0618hrs the Beagle made an emergency crash landing onto Object 556/C.
We sustained severe damage to all controls, engines, and navigational equipment. All raft ships have been damaged.
All eleven crew members survived the impact and are uninjured.
The cargo is intact and operational.
Our initial investigations suggest that **[TEXT MISSING]** previous reports incorrect and **[TEXT MISSING]** the Gyre is inhabited.
We are not alone here.

Report No: 201
Date: 24/12/338ED

[TEXT MISSING] negotiations have failed. Flt Off. Hussein, Dr Kamal, and Lt Siddiqui have been captured and killed.
[TEXT MISSING] unable to repair any of the raft ships, and the clock is counting down towards Day Zero.
[TEXT MISSING] emergency beacon has not

functioned since our second week here.
There seems little hope of rescue.

Report No: 289
Date: 06/03/339ED

Our 100th day on the Gyre has passed
without incident.
[TEXT MISSING] Aisha is recovering
slowly and Dr Heeva remains concerned
by the possibility of infection.
[TEXT MISSING] morale still low after
the attack near the canyon, little over
a week ago. Lts Aziz, Sharma and Saïd
are still missing, presumed dead.
There is a permanent camp near the
copper valleys, in the north, **[TEXT
MISSING]** we can see their fires and hear
their music; a tribal drumming that
mirrors their barbarity.
[TEXT MISSING] both Heeva and Baasim
think we should leave the ship and travel
west, towards the Gyre's edge, but I
disagree.
[TEXT MISSING] and our mission is of
utmost importance.
[TEXT MISSING] just eight days left.
[TEXT MISSING] The humans are coming.

Chapter

1

'**OK. What is that?**' asked Amy, shouting over the shrill bleeping noise that screamed out of the console.

'It's a signal,' the Doctor replied, never once taking his eyes away from the screen before him. 'A beacon. An alarm. No… It's *stranger* than that.'

All at once the TARDIS shook violently, nearly knocking them both off their feet.

'And what was *that*?' said Amy, bracing herself and struggling to keep balance.

'Well, I'm not sure what *that* was,' said the Doctor. 'I think we *may* have hit some sort of gravitational speed bump.'

'A gravitational *speed bump*? They have *speed bumps* in space? How fast were we *going*?'

In the centre of the console, the glowing,

crystalline columns groaned and wheezed, as if wrestling some unimaginable force. The lights began to dim, the interior of the ship descending into gloom.

'Well, not a *speed* bump *as such*,' said the Doctor, completely unfazed by the dimming of the lights and the monstrous cacophony being made by the TARDIS. 'More an abnormality. Smaller than a black hole. *Much* smaller than a black hole. But this is where the signal's coming from.'

There was a sudden terrific clanging sound, like that of a monstrous hammer slamming down onto impossibly large anvil, and the TARDIS stopped moving.

'OK. I think we've landed.' With a knowing grin, the Doctor looked up at Amy for the first time in an age. Though the engines of the TARDIS had stopped wheezing and the outside world was quiet, the inside was still filled with that high-pitched bleeping.

'So is it like a distress signal?' said Amy.

The Doctor nodded. 'That's *exactly* what it's like,' he told her. 'The strange thing is, it's a *trans-temporal* distress signal.'

'Er… English, please?'

'It's a distress signal that crosses time. Very sophisticated, in its own way. A spaceship leaves Planet A and travels to Planet B, six light months away. When it gets to Planet B, something malfunctions. Basically, the distress signal travels *back in time* and reaches Planet A shortly after the spaceship has left, so a rescue party can be organised right away.'

'But if the signal travels back in time, can't they just send the message to themselves to stop them going to Planet B in the first place?'

'Oh, Amy Pond... So much to learn. Paradoxes, space-time, closed time-like loops...'

'OK... So where are we?'

The Doctor beckoned Amy over to his side of the console, and pointed at one of the monitors. Peering at the screen, Amy saw the image of a solar system with twelve planets spreading out from its central star. On the outer edges of the system was a flashing green dot.

The Doctor drew a circle around the screen with his finger tip.

'This is the Battani 045 system. That planet there is Jahi Minor. That planet *there*... well, I can't even *pronounce* the name of *that* planet. That *there* is the comet Schuler-Khan, and *that*...' He pointed at the flashing dot. 'That's us. Thing is... We've landed on something big and solid. And there's nothing big or solid this far out.'

He looked across the console room to the door.

'You want to go out there,' said Amy. It was a statement, not a question.

The Doctor returned his attention to her and

smiled. It was a strange, inscrutable smile that took a second or two to reach his eyes.

'Well,' he said, as he left the console and made his way towards the door with his back to her. 'There *is* a distress signal. I'd be breaching all kinds of intergalactic conduct if I didn't at least *try* and find out where it came from. Plus... big mysterious object which shouldn't be here. It would be lazy not to investigate further, wouldn't it? I mean... Wouldn't it?'

He had opened the door before Amy could reply, and behind his back she rolled her eyes. She had grown accustomed to the Doctor's ways. If there was a mystery on the other side of that door, he was bound to open it.

The Doctor turned around and gestured towards the outside world with both arms, like a magician unveiling his latest trick.

'Come along!' he said, beaming. 'Onwards and upwards!'

Amy ran across the console room and together they made their first, tentative steps outside. The sight that greeted them took Amy's breath away, and the only thing she could do was laugh, more out of disbelief than anything else.

She wasn't quite sure what she had expected. A rocky landscape, perhaps, dotted with craters and mountainous ridges, or a desert. Something a little bit more like the moon. This was nothing like that.

The ground beneath their feet was metal, but neither smooth nor polished. Rather it was composed entirely of flattened scraps of junk; some no bigger than a tin can, others the size of a bus. Stretching out into the distance, this landscape of metal became jagged in places, rising up in crooked hills and spiny, razor-sharp ridges. There were plants here and there, but they were nothing like the plants back home. If it reminded her of anything, the place resembled nothing so much as an endless scrap yard, reaching off as far as the eye could see.

Worst of all was the smell. Amy was reminded of bin day in Leadworth, when the council would come around to collect rubbish, and sometimes, if you were walking behind one of the trucks, you'd find yourself downwind of the most terrible stench. Whatever this world was, it smelled as if it was rotting.

'That's *minging*,' she moaned, pinching her nostrils shut.

'Oh, I don't know,' said the Doctor. 'I've smelled worse. You should try sixteenth-century London. Place was an open sewer. Come along, Pond.'

The Doctor walked out into the metallic valley in which the TARDIS had landed, and, shaking her head in resignation, Amy followed.

'Why do you call me Pond?' she asked, after navigating her way around a particularly tricky mound of crushed steel and twisted plastic.

'Why? Don't you like it?'

'Well… It's just… *Pond*,' said Amy. 'What's wrong with Amy?'

'What was wrong with Amelia?'

'Lots of things. And as for just calling me *Pond*. It makes me sound—'

'Nothing wrong with Pond. I'm quite fond of ponds. Ponds have ducks. Well… Some of them do. And ducks are great. And as for the name… Lots of great people have had the surname Pond. John Pond, for example. Astronomer Royal. Lovely chap. *Filthy* sense of humour, though. Once told me this joke about—'

'Enough about my name,' interrupted Amy. 'What *is* this place? I mean… It's a planet, but you said there shouldn't be any planets here.'

The Doctor stopped walking and looked around at the endless sea of twisted, ancient-looking refuse that surrounded them.

'No,' he said. 'It's not a planet. For one thing, planets aren't flat.'

'What do you mean? How can you tell it's flat?'

'The horizon's all wrong. If I'm not mistaken, and I'm *not*, this place is *flat*. And look… Couple of plants here and there, but the rest is just… well… junk.'

'So… what *is* it?' asked Amy. 'If it's not a planet, what is—'

Before she could finish her question, the Doctor had left her, running further into the valley. Tutting under her breath, Amy chased after him.

'What *now*?' she shouted.

'Oh, you have *got* to be joking!' said the Doctor, as he reached a smaller mound of scrap metal jutting out into their path. With an almost childlike enthusiasm he began lifting smaller fragments, hurling them away. In a flurrying cloud of grey dust, the Doctor had uncovered what looked like a half-buried satellite dish, perhaps two and a half metres in diameter.

'What? What is it?' asked Amy.

'Oh, this is *brilliant*,' the Doctor told her.

'What is?'

Attached to the side of the dish's base was a grubby gold plaque. The Doctor swept his hand across it, clearing away decades, or perhaps even centuries of grime and dust.

'This,' said the Doctor, 'is Pioneer 10.'

Looking over his shoulder Amy saw, engraved on the plaque, an image of a naked man and woman standing before a line drawing of the dish.

'A rude picture?' she said. 'You're looking at a rude picture?'

'It's *not* a rude picture.' The Doctor sighed. 'It's Pioneer 10. Deep-space probe launched by NASA in 1972. So *this* is where it ended up. Quite sad, really.'

'Why has a NASA probe got a rude picture on the side of it?'

'It's *not* a rude…' The Doctor sighed once more. 'It's to show aliens what you lot look like.'

'With our clothes off?'

'Well… *yes*. You're not *born* wearing T-shirt and jeans, are you? Anyway… The idea was that this thing would just keep flying through space, and maybe one day somebody, or some*thing*, would pick it up. Quite sad, really. For it to spend countless millennia travelling across space to just end up on a scrap heap. One great big cosmic scra—'

With a movement so sudden it caused Amy to jump back and almost lose her footing, the Doctor stood up straight and spun around on his heels.

'That's it!' he cried, clicking his fingers. 'That's exactly what this is!'

'What? A scrap heap?'

'Yes! Well, no. Not really. It's junk. Lots of space junk. Gravitational forces, solar winds, pushing and pulling all this junk until it ends up in one place. That's the thing, see? Two thousand centuries of space travel and people are still dropping litter. They'll never learn…'

'Wait. Did you just say two *thousand* centuries?'

'Yes.'

'What year is this?'

'Er… We left Earth in 2010, or thereabouts, yes?'

Amy nodded.

'Well I reckon we're somewhere around the year 250,000.'

Before Amy could say anything, the Doctor crouched down beside the wreckage of the probe once more, flipping open a panel at its side.

'Now where… is… it?' he said, drawing his sonic screwdriver from his pocket with one hand and rummaging through the inside of the probe with the other. 'Oh! There it is!'

With a high-pitched squeal the sonic screwdriver came to life, shining a needle-thin beam of green light into the probe's inner workings.

'Atomic clock.' The Doctor continued. 'Battery's run down a bit since 1972, but this should sort it. Right… Yes. The year is 250,339. To be precise, it's 14 March 250,339. And it's six minutes past one in the afternoon.'

He stood up once more and turned around. Amy was still wide eyed with shock.

'Two… two hundred… and fifty… *thousand*?' she spluttered.

'Three hundred and thirty-nine,' the Doctor added, beaming.

'But that's… that's…'

'Yes. Quite distant future, I suppose. For you.'

'*Quite* distant? *Quite? Distant?*'

'Well, I don't know why you're so surprised. You've been to the *future*. I'd have thought the novelty would have worn off by—'

'But two hundred and fifty *thousand*?'

'Yes. That's what I said. And that would certainly make sense of the *size* of this thing. It must be hundreds, maybe thousands of miles across for it to have any sort of gravity. *And* an atmosphere.'

The Doctor gazed up at the dark blue sky above them. 'Oh! There it is!' he said, grinning and pointing up.

'What's that?' asked Amy.

Following his finger she saw, in amongst the twinkling stars and distant planets, a single glowing object, brighter than anything else. Trailing behind it was a flickering spectral tail, with a faint green and purple mist in its wake.

'Schuler-Khan!' said the Doctor. 'The comet? The one I just mentioned? Only problem is—'

Before he could say another word, they heard the whirring sound of an engine, and a voice shouted, 'Halt!'

Both Amy and the Doctor looked up to the crest of the scrap pile, and saw a four-wheeled vehicle, like a dune buggy. Riding it were two creatures in blue spacesuits, their smooth bald heads a dolphin-like shade of grey, their faces almost featureless save for small black eyes and thin, lipless mouths. Hanging from the side of the vehicle, one of the creatures had a large and powerful-looking rifle aimed straight at them.

'Don't move!' the creature yelled. The engine whirred once more, the large, heavy-duty wheels spinning up clouds of dust and shards of metal, and the buggy came rolling down towards them. After slamming into the Pioneer's dish, crushing it as if it were made of paper, the buggy came to a halt in the valley.

Gesturing to Amy that she should do the same, the Doctor put his hands up.

'Ha!' said the rifle-toting alien. 'Look at this, Charlie. There's only two of them. There are never usually *two* of them. We should take them back.'

The buggy's driver climbed out from behind the steering wheel, looking from the Doctor to Amy, and then back again.

'I don't know, Ahmed,' he said. 'They don't *look* like the others. Look at their clothes.'

'They're *humans*. What else can they be? We should take them back to the ship. Your father'll be happy. Maybe we could use them as hostages. We could bargain with the humans.'

The one called Charlie shook his head. 'No,' he said. 'Humans don't bargain.'

'Er, excuse me...' said Amy, holding one hand higher than the other.

Charlie turned to her. 'Yes?' he snapped.

'Well... I *am* human. And we *do* bargain. Sometimes. I mean... It depends what it's about, really, but...'

'Silence!' said Charlie. 'So you *are* humans? What happened? Get split off from one of your scouting parties, did you? Sent to spy on us? Track us down? Is that it?'

'No!' Amy protested. 'No, we're not spies. We only just got here.' She turned to the Doctor. '*Tell* them.'

'Right, yes…' said the Doctor. 'You see… We picked up a distress signal. Which is why we're here. So you might be just the people we were looking for…'

Charlie shook his head. 'Impossible,' he snapped. 'Our distress signal stopped working two months ago. And *how* did you get here exactly.? If a ship had come in, we would have seen it.'

'Oh, you wouldn't have seen my ship,' the Doctor told him. 'It's only little. Well… On the outside. Plus, it doesn't make much of a song and dance when it turns up. There it is. See? Over there.'

He pointed back in the direction of the TARDIS. Charlie and Ahmed looked to the blue box, dwarfed by its surroundings, and then at one another.

'What *is* that?' asked Ahmed.

'I don't know,' replied Charlie. 'Probably more junk.'

'Hey!' said the Doctor, offended. 'That's not junk, that's the TARDIS.'

Charlie and Ahmed shook their heads in unison.

'All right,' said Ahmed. 'Enough with the games. You're coming with us.' He lifted up his rifle and aimed it at the Doctor, gesturing towards the buggy. 'Get on.'

Giving the TARDIS a final backwards glance, the Doctor nodded reluctantly, and then he and Amy climbed aboard. Amy looked at the Doctor with a scowl. She had expected him to do more than just hold up his hands and surrender like that, but then these aliens did have a gun. A gun that was still aimed at them as Charlie began driving them through the valley and away from the TARDIS.

'Where are you taking us?' asked Amy.

'To our ship,' Ahmed replied coldly. Though his features weren't human, Amy knew an expression of hatred when she saw one.

'Oh, well… this is *exciting*,' said the Doctor. He turned to Amy with a grin, and winked.

Amy laughed incredulously, shaking her head. 'You're crazy,' she said. 'We're *actually* being kidnapped and you're acting like we're on a daytrip to Longleat.'

'Yes,' said the Doctor. 'Cosmic safari. I find it helps when faced with gun-toting aliens. Say… Ahmed…'

Ahmed turned to the Doctor and adjusted his rifle's aim. 'Yes?'

'I couldn't help but notice… That comet. Up there? Schuler-Khan? Is it by any chance—'

His sentence was cut off when, from high above them, they heard a colossal crash. Tumbling down one of the slopes was a flaming ball of refuse, burning fragments breaking away from it as it fell. It landed in their path, only a few feet away from the buggy, and exploded on impact.

Charlie wrenched the steering wheel to one side and the buggy mounted an embankment with a violent shudder. Amy braced herself as best she could, clinging to the back of the driver's seat, but the Doctor was flung clear of the vehicle, rolling back down the embankment and into the valley.

'Doctor!' Amy screamed, as the buggy came to a halt.

Ahmed looked past her, to the ridge from which the fireball had fallen.

'We're under attack!' He shouted, lifting his rifle and firing off several ear-splitting shots into the distance.

Amy's eyes were still on the Doctor, who had landed perhaps six metres away from them. He was dazed, and it took him seconds to gather his senses and get to his feet, but by then it was too late.

There were creatures coming down the hill, creatures dressed in black and dirty rags. They looked, to Amy, like hairless chimpanzees, feral and monstrous, and as they charged down the embankment they hooted and bellowed. She saw one of them armed with a bow and arrow, the tip of which blazed with fire. The missile was launched with terrifying precision and embedded itself, still burning, in the side of the buggy.

'Get us out of here!' shouted Ahmed. 'Quickly!'

Charlie didn't hesitate. The buggy's engine growled to life once more, and then tore up the side of the opposite bank, the wheels skidding from side to side, struggling to grip against the unstable surface.

Amy reached out from the back of the buggy. The Doctor was running after them, away from their attackers, but it was no use. The buggy was too fast, and all too soon the marauders were upon him with rope nets and shackles.

'Stop!' Amy screamed. 'Please! The Doctor. We have to help him!'

But Charlie didn't stop. He carried on driving until they had reached the ridge, and then the buggy was driving down another slope of twisted, ancient metal towards a desert of broken glass.

'No!' Amy cried. 'We have to go back and save him.'

From the driver's seat, Charlie looked at her in one of the rear-view mirrors.

'Save him?' he said. 'What are you talking about? Your friend just got *rescued*. *You're* the one that needs saving.'

Chapter
2

Amy didn't need to be an expert in such matters to know, just by looking at it, that the ship was a wreck. It lay half buried in a landscape of wreckages, more or less camouflaged by the torn and damaged remnants of the older hulls surrounding it. Painted along its side, the letters almost obscured by a layer of black grime and dust, was its name: *BEAGLE XXI.*

They drove in through a small opening where the hull met the ground, and through a labyrinth of low, dark tunnels, until they reached what looked like a loading bay. None of them had spoken in some time.

Ahmed climbed off first, shouldering his rifle. He still looked at Amy with distrust and animosity, and Amy couldn't bring herself to meet his gaze.

'I'll get your father,' said Ahmed to Charlie, before walking out of the bay.

Though she wouldn't admit it out loud, Amy was scared. Terrified, even. She wondered where the Doctor could be, what their attackers could have done with him. What if they *weren't* attackers? What if they *were* just rescuing the Doctor from these aliens? What if she *was* the one who needed rescuing now?

All these thoughts were still racing through her mind when Charlie, still sitting in the front of the buggy, turned around, resting with his arms folded across the top of the driver's seat. 'Are you OK?' he asked.

The question took Amy by surprise. He had seemed so cold, so harsh, when they were driving away from the Doctor. What had changed?

Amy shrugged it off and shook her head.

'This is crazy,' she said, looking at him at last. 'I'm not even meant to be here. This is… this is just *insane*. I mean… Who *are* you? *What* are you?'

Charlie looked at her quizzically, the smooth and shiny grey skin of his forehead creasing up into a frown. 'You don't know who we are?' he asked.

Amy shook her head.

'Well. My name is Baasim al-Jehedeh, but most people call me Charlie. And we are the Sittuun. If that's what you meant.'

'Charlie?' said Amy. 'What kind of an alien name is Charlie? And your mate, there. Ahmed. There was a boy in my school called Ahmed…'

'The Sittuun use human names,' Charlie told her. 'Our language is too complicated for human vocal chords to pronounce and includes frequencies which human ears cannot hear. It's easier for us to adopt Earth names when dealing with Humans…'

'But Sittuun…'

'It's the Arabic word for "sixty",' Charlie explained, and Amy thought she could see his mouth curling up into a smile. 'Our world was first encountered by a Syrian deep-space crew. The first town they came across had sixty inhabitants, so they called us "sittuun". Sixty.'

Amy thought about this for a moment, and then frowned. 'OK,' she said. 'So you lot were discovered by humans…'

'Actually, we prefer the word "encountered".'

'OK. You were *encountered* by humans… You use human names… But you don't *like* humans? And you've kidnapped me because I'm human? And now the Doctor's been captured by those… those *things*… I mean, what *were* they?'

'You mean you don't know?' said Charlie.

Before he could say any more, they heard the sound of marching feet in an outside corridor, and they were joined by Ahmed and another Sittuun. This one, Amy noticed, had a heavier build than either Charlie or Ahmed, and along the dome of his head was a thin, Mohawk-like strip of white hair. His uniform looked military, with coloured stripes along the breast pocket of his jacket. He turned to Charlie, and began speaking in a series of high-pitched whistles and loud clicks. Charlie shrank away from the older-looking Sittuun, almost cowering.

'I don't get it,' said Amy. 'The Doctor told me that the TARDIS would translate anything people said. Anything. Anywhere.'

The older Sittuun looked at her with an expression of condescension and shook his head.

'Dad…' said Charlie awkwardly. 'Speak human, please. We have a guest.'

'We have a *prisoner*, Baasim,' snapped his father. He turned to Amy. 'What kind of translation were you expecting, girl? Vocal modulator? Telepathic field? Those things don't work on our language. Tell me… Who *are* you? Where did you come from? The human city?'

'My name's Amy Pond,' said Amy. 'I'm from Leadworth. It's near Gloucester.'

'Gloucester? What is Gloucester?'

'It's a town.'

'But *where*?'

'Er… Planet Earth?'

'You're from Earth? *Planet* Earth? You *know* that you're from Earth?'

'Er... *Yes?* I'm human, and I'm from Earth. Is that so weird?'

The three Sittuun looked at one another in surprise.

'Remarkable,' said Charlie's father, his tone still hesitant and condescending. 'Well, isn't that something? She might just be telling the truth.' He turned to Amy once more. 'I am Captain Jamal al-Jehedeh of the *Beagle XXI*. Follow me, Amy Pond. I'd like to know how you ended up here.'

Amy sat on the edge of a bed in the medical bay while another Sittuun, who introduced herself as Dr Heeva, inspected her for cuts and bruises. They had given her a bowl of soup that tasted strangely of chemicals but not food, and the four of them now stood around her, looking at her as if she were a sideshow exhibit or an animal in a zoo.

'It's certainly far-fetched,' said Captain Jamal to Dr Heeva. 'I mean... Time machines. Alien Time Lords. Space whales. Intergalactic felons. What do you think?'

'Possibly concussion,' replied Heeva. 'But she's not like the others, is she? She doesn't *look* like them. She doesn't *talk* like them.'

'Er, hello?' said Amy, waving her hand in the air. 'I'm still here?'

The four Sittuun looked at her with something resembling embarrassment.

'So,' she continued, 'I've given you my life story in a nutshell. How about you lot? What are you doing here? And what is this place, anyway?'

'This is Object 556/C,' said Captain Jamal. 'But we call it the Gyre. It's been here for maybe three thousand centuries. Shipwrecks and refuse brought together by the gravitational force of the five nearest stars.'

'Gravitational forces!' Amy said with a smile. 'That's what the Doctor said!'

'The Doctor?' asked the Captain.

'Her friend,' explained Charlie. He lowered his voice. 'He was the one taken by the humans.'

'Ah. I see. Well, yes, as I was saying, the Gyre has been here for three hundred thousand Earth years, at least. Growing bigger and bigger, year after year. It's only posed a problem in recent months. Ships passing near it began encountering navigational problems. The gravitational force of the Gyre itself is beginning to have an effect on the nearest planet's orbit. And then there's the comet...'

'Schuler-Khan?'

Captain Jamal frowned at Amy and then nodded. 'Yes,' he said, sounding vaguely surprised. 'That's right. Schuler-Khan. Now... Schuler-Khan's orbit around Battani 045 lasts eighty-five years, and on previous occasions it has missed the Gyre altogether. But not this time. The gravitational pull has changed the comet's course and, in only a few hours' time, Schuler-Khan will crash straight into the Gyre. Which is why we're here.'

Amy sat on the bed, dumbstruck for a moment. She put down the bowl of soup and leaned forward. 'You mean to tell me you *came* here just to see it get hit by a great big comet?'

Captain Jamal shook his head. 'No, not at all. We came here to *destroy* the Gyre. If Schuler-Khan hits the Gyre it will send chunks of debris the size of cities spinning off through space. There are twelve inhabited worlds within twenty-five million miles, including our own. The impact on them will be devastating. Our mission was to detonate a Nanobomb in the Gyre's upper atmosphere, thereby neutralising the threat.'

'A Nanobomb?' Amy winced. 'That doesn't sound good.'

'It's fine, really,' said Charlie, trying to sound reassuring. 'It releases Nanites which eat up all the metal and plastic in a matter of seconds. Eventually all that's left is atoms. The Nanites even destroy *themselves*.'

'So what went wrong?'

'We crashed,' said Captain Jamal. 'As we were nearing the Gyre our systems crashed, and then so did this ship.' He paused, looking down at the tiled floor of the med bay. 'We thought there was nothing here,' he went on. 'Ships had been passing this thing for millennia. No one thought it was inhabited. No one thought it *could* be. There were no signs of life. But then we got here…'

Dr Heeva stepped in, looking at Amy directly. 'They must have been shipwrecked,' she said. 'Thousands of years ago. Hundreds of thousands, maybe.'

'Who? Who were shipwrecked?'

Captain Jamal looked up at her, his expression solemn. 'The ones who kidnapped your friend,' he replied. 'The humans.'

Chapter
3

The gully was dark and narrow. To either side, two walls of scrap rose up, cutting down the dark blue sky to a narrow sliver and, every so often, small fragments of metal would come tumbling down into their path, kicking up clouds of dust.

The Doctor's wrists were bound tight in front of him with a thick and grubby length of rope. One of the humans walked behind, the tip of his spear trained right between the Doctor's shoulder blades, its sharpened point nudging him whenever he walked a little slower.

Eventually the canyon opened out onto the edge of a vast gorge, perhaps two hundred metres across, and unfathomably deep. Crossing the ravine was what looked, at first, like an enormous metal bridge. Only as they got closer could the Doctor recognise it as a pipe, ten metres or so in diameter. It was ancient, its rusting trunk draped with creeping green vines.

'That's the exhaust off a Proamonian dreadnaught...' said the Doctor. 'Do you know something? You could make a *fortune* recycling this place. You know, Proamonians only ever built their ships out of proamonium? Rarest mineral in the universe, proamonium. Only found on Proamon, funnily enough.'

'Silence!' shouted the human with the spear. 'You do not speak.'

The Doctor looked back to see his malevolent glare, and the human bared his teeth, grunting and snarling, and nudging the Doctor once more with his spear.

'Ah!' the Doctor gasped. 'Easy... easy... That's actually quite painful, you know.'

They were crossing the pipe now, the sound of their marching clanging and echoing beneath them. To either side of this makeshift bridge, the gorge descended into complete darkness, its depths enshrouded in a perpetual gloom.

The Doctor looked around at his captors and sighed. How long had they *been* here, on this floating disc of space junk? They were human, he could tell that much, but he doubted any human being on Earth would recognise them as their own.

At the other end of the bridge they entered a murky swamp of dark green sludge, from which emerged hundreds, if not thousands, of corrugated plastic tubes, like an artificial bamboo forest. The humans, the Doctor noticed, were growing edgy and cautious, and they made their way into the swamp with slow, deliberate steps. All around them the plastic tubes dipped and swayed, chiming against one another like percussion instruments, and the stagnant breeze sang over their open necks like a ghostly choir.

From nearby they heard a sudden heavy splash, and everybody froze.

'Sollog,' whispered one of the humans, his eyes darting from side to side.

'Sollog,' said another, drawing a battered-looking sword from its scabbard.

'Er... Who... or *what* is Sollog?' asked the Doctor, but nobody answered him.

There was another splash, and now he heard something else. Something guttural and animalistic, almost like a belch, or the sound of a bullfrog.

Another splash. And then another.

The human with the sword was turning now, searching desperately for the source of those sounds, his expression one of outright terror. His hands shook as he gripped the weapon's handle and his jaw was trembling.

'What's Sollog?' the Doctor asked, more

insistently now, but the human didn't answer him. He was looking over the Doctor's shoulder, his eyes growing wide and his mouth opening for a scream he'd never start.

The creature that leapt on him was at least a metre long, the trunk of its body like that of a monstrous slug, and its eyes jutted out on slimy stalks. Unlike a slug, it propelled itself on eight long and spindly legs, which protruded from its sides.

It struck the human with such force that it pushed him down under the water in a split second, its legs wrapped around his head and upper body. The stricken man thrashed around under the surface of the swamp, but nobody would help him.

More of the creatures, the Sollogs, were emerging from the fetid green waters of the swamp. They climbed the plastic tubes and propelled themselves along with terrifying agility. One of the humans hit one with a shot from his crossbow, but was then taken down when another of the creatures leapt onto his back; its gaping maw filled with circular rows of sharp teeth opening wide above his head.

Without a moment's hesitation, the humans began running further into the swamp, the plastic tubes chiming around them. The Doctor ran as best he could with his hands still tied, but then he heard a heavy splash. He turned round and saw the human who had nudged him along with a spear lying face down in the water.

Crouching, and with a great deal of difficulty, the Doctor grabbed the human by the arm and turned him over. The human coughed up a mouthful of water, wriggled free of the Doctor's grasp, and began searching in the swamp for his spear.

The rest of the group were far away now, still running through the forest of plastic tubes, their yelling and screaming getting quieter by the second. The Doctor and his captor were alone, but for the Sollogs, which were drawing around them in an ever-tightening circle.

'Cut the rope,' said the Doctor, holding up his bound wrists.

The human shook his head.

'Cut the rope or we are going to *die*,' insisted the Doctor.

The human looked around at the seven or eight Sollogs that were crawling and slithering from one pipe to the next. He turned to the Doctor and, drawing a small knife from his belt, proceeded to hack through the rope, freeing the Doctor's hands. The Doctor reached inside his jacket, and the human flinched, holding the blade a little closer to his face.

'Easy... easy...' said the Doctor, drawing out his sonic screwdriver.

Close by, one of the Sollogs let out a terrifying hiss. The human jumped, but the Doctor remained calm, grabbing the nearest plastic tube, and placing the tip of the screwdriver against its corrugated shell. As the device chirruped into life there came, from the open mouth of the pipe, a deafening, bass-heavy drone. The Doctor pulled down the pipe, holding it under his arm as if it were a gun, and aimed it at the Sollogs. The throbbing sound pulsated out of the pipe, causing everything in its path to quiver and shake, and the Sollogs began screeching and mewling, before scurrying away from them.

The Doctor let out a brief, almost nervous laugh, as if amazed his plan had worked. Then, when the Sollogs were a safe distance away, he grabbed the human by his wrist, and dragged him off across the swamp.

'What was *that*?' asked the human, breathlessly.

'That was improvisation,' the Doctor replied. 'And all things considered, I think it went rather well.'

Eventually they were clear of the swamp and racing across a glittering white desert. Behind them the Sollogs clung to the swaying plastic tubes, but they came no further. Turning on his heels the Doctor watched them massing at the edges of the swamp, hissing and screeching. Why weren't they still chasing them? He looked down at the crunchy white crystals at his feet.

'Salt,' he realised. 'It's a *salt plain*.'

He would have smiled with relief were he not thinking about Amy. Amy Pond, who was somewhere, far beyond the swamp and the canyon. Alone on a world as dangerous as this. He had to get back to her, somehow, but his thoughts were interrupted as he felt his wrists pressed together, and the all-too-familiar sensation of rough rope being tied around them. The human he had just saved was binding them together once more, and had the tip of his dagger pointed towards the Doctor's face.

'Oh, well that's just *charming*,' said the Doctor. 'And I thought we were friends.'

'You are not my friend,' grunted the human. 'You are my prisoner. Now start walking.'

They made their way towards those who had escaped from the swamp moments before them. In the distance, beyond the rest of the group, the Doctor saw a dark shape rising up against the perpetual night, an enormous hulk that shimmered at first, like a mirage. Only as they drew nearer did he recognise it as the wreckage of a spaceship.

Though it was half buried in the surface, it rose up a quarter of a mile from the ground, like an iron finger pointing at the sky. Along its side was painted a single word, GOBO, and next to it the image of a cartoon clown with bright blue hair and a crimson, rictus grin.

As they neared the hulk, the Doctor heard the

sound of drumming and saw blazing torches lined up along fortified ramparts. All around the wreck there were makeshift buildings: tin shacks and huts; ramshackle turrets and cobbled-together shelters – a city made of junk. A fanfare of discordant, atonal horns greeted them from the watchtowers along the city's outer walls, and the doors of an immense iron gate groaned open. The drumming grew louder still as they approached, passing through the gate and into the city, and then the doors slammed shut behind them with a heavy clang.

When they saw him, the humans in the city began to hoot and bellow, jumping up and down and beating their chests. A small child, its eyes glowing with feral intensity, ran up to the Doctor and kicked him in the leg. Another threw a clod of dirt at his head, narrowly missing him. His captors shooed them away with their spears, and took him further into the city.

The buildings that surrounded them looked impossibly ancient and run-down, as if they had been fashioned as emergency shelters in a crisis, many centuries ago, but had since fallen into disrepair. The rooftops were rusted and sagging, columns bowing beneath their weight. The whole place stank of smoke and rotting food.

They came at last to the upturned hull of an old deep-space shuttle. Its shell, which would once have been white and emblazoned with the livery of whichever space agency had sent it, was now painted, from end to end, with primitive graffiti. Over and over again, the Doctor saw a childish interpretation of the clown's grinning face.

A door in the shuttle's hull swung open with a gasp, and a human climbed out: a short man with long, greasy black hair cascading down his hunched back like a river of tar. One side of his face was tattooed with tiger patterns and his features were pinched and rat-like. He walked with the assistance of a gnarled black staff, at the top of which was a human skull. On seeing the Doctor he laughed in a series of short, staccato cackles, clasping his hands together with glee. His fingernails were long, brown talons.

'Ah, Sancho…' he rasped. 'What do we have here?'

'We have a prisoner, Tuco,' said Sancho, the human soldier who the Doctor had saved. 'We caught him.'

'Yes. A prisoner. Yes,' hissed the tattooed human. 'Yes. Tuco likes this very much. Yes. A *prisoner*.'

Tuco approached the Doctor now, inspecting him from head to toe. He reached out, dragging one of his claw-like fingers the length of the Doctor's face, from his forehead to his chin, and the Doctor followed the course of his finger with his eyes but remained stoic.

'Ha ha!' cackled Tuco. 'He has a funny face! But

he's not Sittuun, no?'

'He was with the Sittuun,' said Sancho.

'*With* Sittuun? With Sittuun. Yes. With Sittuun. Are you a friend of the Sittuun?'

The Doctor shrugged. 'Well... I'm quite easy to get along with, I think. So... Tuco...'

Tuco recoiled, as if he had been stung. He frowned at the Doctor.

'He speaks!'

'Yes, I *speak*. So... Tuco, as I was about to say before you had your little... ah, *moment* there... How long have you guys been here?'

The humans looked at one another, frowning.

'What does he mean?' asked Sancho.

'Yes, stranger. Yes. Tuco would like to know. What do you mean?'

'Well... This place. How long have there been humans here? When were you shipwrecked? That's assuming you *were* shipwrecked, and you didn't come here by choice. I mean, I *love* what you've done with the place, really, but still... It's not exactly a holiday resort, is it?'

'Silence!' Tuco roared. 'He speaks the heresy!'

The humans gasped, clasping their hands over their ears.

'I'm sorry,' said the Doctor. 'Did I just say something?'

Tuco leaned close to him now, his dark green eyes glowing with intent.

'We have *always* been here,' he snarled, baring his yellow, misshapen teeth. 'There is no shipwreck.'

The Doctor was gazing up now, at the broken hull of the GOBO ship.

'Er... Excuse me?' he said. 'But... Where exactly do you think you *are*?'

'This,' said Tuco, grinning ominously, 'is Earth. And you, stranger, are a heretic.' He turned to the Doctor's captors. 'Take him away,' he hissed. 'Django will decide his fate.'

Chapter

4

'But... I saw those things... They weren't human.'

Amy was following Charlie along one of the Sittuun ship's corridors, though she had no idea where he was going.

'They were,' said Charlie. 'I'm sorry.'

'But what *happened* to them?'

They came at last to a control room lined with banks of monitors. Charlie sat at one of the consoles and started typing. After a moment he paused, turning round in his chair.

'We don't know how long they've been here. It could be thousands of years. They're most likely the descendents of a crew who were shipwrecked here. They've forgotten everything. Their technology, or most of it. Their history.'

'But they don't even *look* human.'

'Well, they *do*,' said Charlie. 'If you're Sittuun, I mean. Most of you kind of… well… you all kind of look the same, really.' He frowned and shook his head. 'I'm sorry,' he said. 'That's really racist, isn't it?'

Amy couldn't help but laugh. 'Well, yeah… Kinda.' Her expression became more grave. 'But what about the Doctor? If they've got him… What will they *do* to him?'

Charlie shrugged and hung his head. 'I don't know,' he said. 'They killed three of our crew when we first landed, and they captured another three a few weeks back. We haven't seen them since. There were eleven of us. Aisha… she was our chief navigator… She died after being bitten by one of the Sollogs. So now there's just us four.'

'And how long have you been here?'

Charlie closed his small black eyes and sighed. 'One hundred and eight days,' he told her. 'We've been here a hundred and eight days. We're trying to salvage one of the raft ships, but the Gyre has scrambled all of the ship's navigational programmes. Even if we *could* get one of the rafts to fly – and we *can't* – it could send us anywhere. We could be floating in deep space for centuries.'

Amy sat down at the console next to Charlie and put her head in her hands. When she looked up at him again it was with a quizzical scowl. 'But what I don't understand is, why didn't you just fire a great big missile across space to blow this place up? Why did you have to come here?'

'The Gyre,' Charlie replied. 'It's strange. It's like it has a mind of its own. Like it's *conscious*. It causes all kinds of problems. The only way to destroy it was to do it up close.'

'And there's just you guys? And just the one bomb? Why isn't there a whole *fleet* of ships with lots of bombs out there?'

Charlie laughed. 'A whole fleet?' he said. 'With *lots* of bombs? Nanobombs aren't cheap, and the one on this ship is the largest that's ever been manufactured. It took the combined funds of eight planets in the Battani system, with emergency aid from another *fifteen* worlds to buy just *one* bomb. That's why today is our last chance. And so far, it's not looking good.'

'But the Doctor...' said Amy with a troubled look. 'If he was here he'd know what to do.'

She could feel an anger rising up from the pit of her stomach.

'If you hadn't kidnapped us, we could have *helped* you.'

'What do you mean?' asked Charlie.

'His ship. The TARDIS. It can take you *anywhere* in the universe. We could have got you out of here. But the Doctor's the only one who can fly it, and now he's gone.'

Charlie sat back in his chair, covering his face with his hands. He uttered something in Sittuun, something blunt and guttural.

'Did you just *swear*?' asked Amy.

Charlie nodded. 'We didn't *know*,' he said. 'You both looked like *them*. If we'd just brought you back here, and you'd offered to take us away in that DARTIS—'

'TARDIS.'

'Sorry... *TARDIS*. If you'd come here and told us that, my father would never have believed you. He really doesn't like humans. Many Sittuun don't.'

Amy was surprised. In her lifetime she had heard people say insulting things about women, Scottish people and redheads, and sometimes she would take offence. She'd never imagined feeling offended on behalf of her entire *species*.

'Why not?' she asked.

'Because,' Charlie said, trying to sound as tactful as he could, 'humans are superstitious, unpredictable and violent. You were an apex predator on Earth, and you spread it around wherever you go. Back on our home world, before humans turned up, there *were* no predators. Can you imagine that? Not a single carnivorous life form on the entire planet. Quite rare, apparently. But do you know something? It means we evolved without fear. Without fear, there *is* no superstition. We have no myths, no religions, no monsters in our closets. But *humans*... You're scared of absolutely *everything*. And look where it's got you.'

'And what's *that* supposed to mean?'

Charlie turned away. 'The first three... the ones they killed,' he said, his voice a little softer. 'They went to the human city to warn them about the comet. We were offering to save them. And the humans... they just didn't *care*. They didn't want to *know*, or *listen*. They hung the bodies at the city gates for us to see, and then they came for us. We've been hiding out here ever since. So if you want to know why my father doesn't like humans... well... there's your answer.'

Amy nodded, feeling a sudden sympathy for Charlie and the others, and a terrible fear for the Doctor.

'We aren't *all* like them,' she said, sounding almost apologetic.

Charlie smiled at her. 'I know,' he said. 'I know.'

'So what can we do?' asked Amy. 'I can't just *sit* here and do *nothing*. Those humans have the Doctor. God knows what they've done to him...'

'There's nothing we *can* do,' said Charlie desolately. 'In a few hours Schuler-Khan is going to crash into the Gyre. We either sit here and wait for it to happen, or we detonate the Nanobomb and get atomised. Sorry, Amy... There's no fairy-tale happy ending.'

He was looking at her again with a soulful expression when, from beyond the control room, they heard hurried, clanking footsteps. The door crashed open, and Ahmed burst into the room, skidding to a halt. He braced himself with both hands clasping his knees and gasping for breath, his cheeks flushed a strange shade of turquoise.

'Come quickly!' he said, still breathless. 'We've got an incoming ship. Looks like an Earth vessel.'

Amy and Charlie looked at one another and were on their feet and running in a fraction of a second, following Ahmed down the corridor to the bridge. Captain Jamal and Dr Heeva were waiting for them.

'Look!' Ahmed said, pointing up at the sky.

Sure enough, streaking across the sapphire-coloured skies above the Gyre was a single, small spacecraft. Its hull was a vibrant yellow with a single red stripe from its nose cone to its tailfins. It looked, to Amy, more like the kind of spaceship she had seen in cartoons when she was younger than the industrial and functional ships she had encountered in her travels so far.

The yellow ship banked sharply to its left, and they could hear its rockets shuddering and wheezing. It was heading straight for them.

'It's going to hit us!' cried Dr Heeva.

The Sittuun all hit the deck, and Amy followed suit, covering her face with her hands and squinting up at the windows through the gaps between her fingers. The ship was coming closer, bearing down on them but, when it was only a hundred metres or so away, it stopped very suddenly. Turning slowly on its axis, the yellow craft shook in mid air, clouds of black smoke belching out of its vents, and slowly began its descent.

Amy and the others got to their feet and watched as it landed with a heavy thump in a dense cloud of dust.

'It's a ship,' breathed Ahmed, his hands and face pressed up against the window.

'Yes, Corporal Ahmed, we can see that,' said Captain Jamal.

'No...' said Ahmed, turning around to face them. 'I mean, it's a *ship*. We're rescued! We're actually rescued!'

Before Captain Jamal could say anything further, Ahmed and Charlie had raced out from the bridge. After a second's hesitation, Amy, Captain Jamal and Dr Heeva followed them.

'It just *had* to be humans, didn't it?' said the Captain. 'And you know, we'll never hear the last of it.'

'Quite,' said Dr Heeva. 'And of course, the way they'll talk about it, it won't just be *us* these humans saved. It'll be the whole flipping *galaxy*.'

Amy scowled at Dr Heeva and the Captain, and followed after Ahmed and Charlie as they ran down several flights of stairs to the loading bay's entrance. Ahmed was carrying his rifle.

'Well…' he said, noticing Amy's disapproving glare, 'you never know, eh?'

They left the hull of the *Beagle XXI* and ran out across the plain to where the yellow spaceship had landed. Written in dashing calligraphy along its hull was the ship's name: *The Golden Bough*.

For a moment, Amy and the crew of the *Beagle* stood around the ship, gazing up at it in silenced awe. Under the very thin veil of dust that had coated it upon landing, its canary-coloured hull still shone. It could not have looked more incongruous, in the bleak and barren landscape of the Gyre; like a glittering diamond in a mound of coal.

When a door in the hull hissed open, all five of them jumped and took a step back. The door lowered itself with hydraulic grace, revealing a flight of gleaming chrome steps, and there was a moment's pause before there appeared, at the top of the stairs, a man in a shining silver spacesuit. Faced by Amy and the Sittuun, all of them covered in grey dust, the new arrival looked strangely glamorous and unfazed. He ran down the steps, his beaming smile revealing perfectly white teeth. His hair was styled in a way that reminded Amy of the kind of film stars she had seen in old movies, and his upper lip was adorned with a thin and rakish moustache.

'Afternoon!' said the stranger, as he stepped down onto the Gyre.

The Sittuun looked at one another, then Amy, and then back to the stranger, who walked straight up to Captain Jamal, holding out his hand.

'Dirk Slipstream at your service,' he said. 'You must be Captain Jamal al-Jehedeh. Am I correct?'

Captain Jamal nodded. 'You are,' he said, a little awkwardly.

'Jolly good. So… Seems you chaps have run into a spot of bother.' Dirk Slipstream gazed up at the wreck of the *Beagle XXI*. 'Blimey. She's looking a bit worse for wear, what?'

'I'm sorry,' said Captain Jamal. 'But… who… *are* you?'

Slipstream's gaze snapped back to the Captain, his eyes growing wide. He looked offended in some way.

'I'm Dirk Slipstream,' he said, as if that were explanation enough. 'Formerly of the Terran Airborne Division. Won four Silver Buzzards at the Battle Of Krontep?'

Captain Jamal said nothing.

'Well, anyway,' Slipstream continued, 'I've gone freelance. Search and rescue mainly. Heard you fellas were having some trouble out here in the back of beyond, so thought I'd come and offer you a lift out of here.'

'That's… that's brilliant,' said Dr Heeva.

Though Amy wasn't even sure if they could, she thought the Sittuun doctor was about to cry.

'Excellent,' said Slipstream. 'Well, chaps and chapesses… You'd best get your bags packed. You are being rescued!'

Charlie and Ahmed cheered, and Captain Jamal and Dr Heeva gently embraced one another.

'But…' said Amy. 'What about the Doctor?'

The Sittuun turned to face her, their expressions grave.

'What?' said Slipstream. 'Doctor? Which Doctor?'

'He's my friend,' said Amy. 'And the humans kidnapped him. They've still got him.'

'Humans, you say?'

'Yes. There are humans here, but they're not… they're not like *us*. They're different. They captured the Doctor and they took him away.'

Slipstream thought on this a moment, pacing back and forth in the dust and stroking his chin between forefinger and thumb.

'Humans, eh?' he said eventually. 'Must be that settlement I passed when I was coming in to land. Few miles east of here, if you can call it east. Blasted thing's as flat as a pancake and twice as round. Most confounding. So who's this Doctor chappy then, eh?'

'Like I said… He's my friend. And he's my only way home.'

Slipstream nodded sympathetically. 'I see,' he said. 'Well… I do hate to see a young filly all upset. Breaks a chap's heart.'

'What are you saying?' asked Captain Jamal, suddenly concerned. 'You're not seriously thinking of—'

'My dear Captain, back where I'm from we have a little thing called *honour*. If there's a poor chap being held by those savages, it's my job to rescue him. Now who's with me?'

Slipstream turned to face Charlie, Ahmed and Amy. The younger Sittuun looked at one another.

'We should,' said Charlie.

Ahmed didn't seem so sure. 'Really? But we could just fly out of here. Right now. We could be gone. We'd never have to see this place again…'

'But we left him there,' said Charlie, looking across at Amy. 'Her friend. And he could have helped us, but we left him there.'

Amy didn't have to think twice about it. She turned to Slipstream. 'I'm in,' she said.

'Jolly good. Now, the only trouble is, the *Golden Bough* won't take us out that far. The magnetic pole here plays havoc with her navigation. We'll have to go on foot. Best get everything you need, and we'll be off in a jiffy. Yes?'

Captain Jamal began shaking his head. 'No,' he said. 'No, this is *insane*. Mr Slipstream—'

'You can call me Dirk, old chap.'

Captain Jamal huffed. 'Dirk… In a few hours' time a comet will smash into this world. Our mission is to destroy the Gyre before that happens. We do not have the *time* for you to launch some half-baked rescue mission. You have a working ship. Let's activate the Nanobomb and get *out of here.*'

Slipstream raised one eyebrow laconically. 'Steady on, old chap,' he said. 'Y'see… The thing I've learned over the years, Captain, is that there's nothing like bad press to ruin a man's career. Let me explain… When we get off this barren, godforsaken world and back to civilisation, do you really want to be the man who left a fellow traveller to die in the clutches of those brutes? Do you? No. I thought not. Now you run along and gather your belongings. I'm rescuing the Doctor.'

Chapter
5

From the upturned shuttle near the city gates, the Doctor was taken by his captors down into a subterranean network of damp, dark tunnels.

They came eventually to a wrought-iron gate guarded by a short, plump man with a face like a bulldog.

'Who is this?' grunted the guard.

'He is a heretic,' replied Sancho. 'Tuco says to put him in a cell. Django will deal with him later.'

The guard nodded and grunted once more and opened the gate. They took the Doctor through into the city's dungeons, the guard waddling in front of them, his heavy bulk shifting from side to side as he walked.

'Say, Sancho,' said the Doctor.

Sancho looked across at the Doctor, his eyebrows furrowed.

'What?'

'We made a good team, didn't we? Earlier on? Us versus the Sollogs?'

Sancho scowled at the Doctor. 'No team,' he snapped. 'You were a prisoner.'

'Yes, but still… The look on their faces… well, if you can call them *faces*… when I did the old trick with the pipe? That was *priceless*. Wasn't it?'

Sancho's expression softened, and the Doctor was sure that for just one second he saw the traces of a smile beginning to appear.

They came eventually to a vaulted chamber filled with individual prison cells, and the guard began rattling his truncheon along the bars.

'Man-co!' he sang, tauntingly. 'Maaan-co! Hey, Wordslinger… We've got a friend for you.'

The Doctor looked through into one of the cells and saw a man sitting on a low cot with his head in his hands. He was wearing an ill-fitting navy blue blazer with tarnished brass buttons; a jacket that clearly hadn't been tailored for the wearer. The man looked up, straight at the Doctor, and smiled weakly.

'He's a heretic, just like you, Manco!' leered the guard. He unclipped a ring of keys from his belt and unlocked the cell opposite Manco's. 'Get in,' he snarled, and the Doctor did as he was told.

The door was slammed shut with a loud clang and, locking it, the guard peered in at the Doctor with a toothless grin and laughed through his nose. Sancho gave the Doctor one last look, a puzzled frown, and then they left.

When he was sure they were far from the dungeon, the Doctor surreptitiously drew his sonic screwdriver from his pocket and aimed it at the lock. It chirruped and squealed, its thin green beam illuminating the lock, but nothing happened. He'd thought as much. Some locks were just too old and too alien for even his trusty screwdriver. Looking up, he saw his fellow prisoner looking across the dungeon at him from his cell.

'What… what *is* that?' asked Manco.

'This?' said the Doctor, holding up the sonic screwdriver. 'Oh… This is just a screwdriver. Though what I wouldn't give for a file in a cake right now…'

'You aren't one of us,' said Manco.

'No. No… You could say I'm not from round these parts.'

Manco smiled. 'And you're a heretic, they say?' he asked, a note of optimism and hope creeping into his voice.

'Well… So they tell me,' said the Doctor. 'Not quite sure what I've done to earn the title, though. How about you? What did you say to get yourself banged up in here?'

Manco leaned to one side, peering out through the bars to check that the coast was clear. 'I questioned the Story,' he said.

'The Story? Which story?'

'The Story of Earth.'

'Right,' said the Doctor. 'Only, you see… that's the thing. This *isn't* Earth. You do know that. Don't you?'

Manco shrugged. 'I'm not sure any more. When I was a child, maybe. They would tell us the Story, and I believed every word of it, but now…'

'OK. Well… You've got me. I am *literally* a captive audience. What's "the Story of Earth"?'

Gazing up at the ceiling, and speaking as if from some long-remembered recitation, Manco spoke:

'In the beginning was the dark blue night and the silence and the empty and the none. Into this came Gobo, and He said, "There shall be a world here in this dark blue night and I shall call it Earth." And He created the Earth out of all the things the Olden Ones had left behind, and into the Earth He put mankind, and He created plants so that they might breathe, and animals so that they might eat, and water that they might drink. And around His tower He built a city in which they might live, and He made the salt plains to guard against the Sollogs in the West. And to this day Gobo looks down upon creation from His tower, and the people of this Earth wait for the day of His return, when He shall take them to the land of El Paso.'

Manco looked at the Doctor and nodded, clearly satisfied that he had remembered it word for word. 'There *is* more,' he said. 'But that's how it starts.'

The Doctor was silent for a moment.

'El Paso?' he said, at last. 'As in El Paso, Texas?'

'Yes. You've *heard* of it?'

'Heard of it? I've *been* there…'

Manco shook his head. 'No,' he said. 'That isn't possible. The Story says that only when we have proven ourselves here on Earth will Gobo take us to El Paso.'

'No, Manco… listen… El Paso is *on* Earth. This *isn't* Earth. This… this is a great big disc of space junk on the outer edges of the Battani system. It's *not* Earth. But you know that already, don't you?'

Manco held the bars of his cell, and stared down at the stone floor, nodding sheepishly.

'Tell me, Manco… What do *you* know? Why have they locked you up?'

Manco was now pacing around the cell, fidgeting and scratching his head. 'Inside the tower,' he said, his voice hushed and timid. 'I went into the tower. *Nobody* goes into the tower, but Django sent me there. When the great star appeared again. He sent me there to look for information. Anything that might tell us what it meant.'

'The great star? You mean the comet? The one that's in the sky right now?'

Manco nodded. 'Yes. The Star Of The Green Tail. So I went into the tower, deep into its heart, but I found nothing about the star.'

The human fell silent. He sat on the edge of his cot with his head in his hands, and the Doctor could hear him breathing, each breath shaking with emotion, as if he was about to cry.

'What did you find, Manco? What was in the tower?'

Manco looked up at the Doctor, shaking his head as if he dared not believe what he was about to say.

'They had screens,' he said. 'Like the one in the Chamber of Stories, but made of glass, and there were hundreds of them. I tried to make them work, to make the pictures happen, but there was nothing. There was no power. I found papers, documents, in a room deep inside the tower. The things I read... the things that had been written down... his name...'

'Whose name?'

Manco looked across the dungeon, staring straight at the Doctor. 'His name was Zachary Velasquez of the Gobocorp Freight Company. He was the captain of the ship. His words said there had been three thousand of them, before they crashed. But then, after the crash, there were just five hundred. They were so scared, he said. All of them. So far away from *home*. From *Earth*.'

The Doctor stumbled back from the bars of his cell and fell into his cot, barely able to look at Manco, let alone speak to him. Though he had guessed at such an explanation for the humans' presence here, it felt suddenly so much more real to him. Perhaps it was knowing the name of the ship's captain, or that there were just five hundred survivors from the crash. Whatever it was, the cold, stark reality of it hit him in a juggernaut of emotion. He wondered how long it had taken the humans who had crashed here, employees of the intergalactic freight company Gobocorp, to give up all hope. How much longer for them to forget where they had come from? How much longer still for them to take the company's mascot – that grinning cartoon clown on the ship's hull – and turn it into a god?

'It's true, isn't it?' Manco said at last. 'This is *not* Earth. We came from… somewhere else, didn't we?'

The Doctor looked up at him and nodded. 'It's true,' he said. 'The tower that you went into… That was the ship. It was a freighter, carrying cargo from one end of the galaxy to the other. You are the descendents of the surviving crew.'

'And what about Gobo…?'

The Doctor sighed. How could he explain this without breaking Manco's heart?

'Gobo was a symbol,' he said softly. 'A drawing.

Something made up by people on Earth. He isn't real.'

The human was now hunched over in his cot, sobbing. 'I knew it,' he said. 'And I told Django... about the words I had read, the Captain's words. Django told me it was a trick, a trick placed here by the Bad.'

'The Bad? Who's the Bad?'

'The enemy of Gobo. The dark one who is the enemy of mankind. The speaker of lies. Django said it was the *Bad* who sent the grey people from the sky, the ones who called themselves *Sittuun*. The Bad put those things inside the tower, to confuse us, but I knew he was lying.'

'Did you try telling the others?'

'I didn't have a chance. Django had me thrown in this place. Nobody else is allowed into the tower, and I'm the only one left who can read or write the language of the Olden Ones. It's the only reason I'm still alive.'

'You're the only one who can read or write?'

Manco nodded, and then, speaking once more as if remembering a passage of scripture:

'And Gobo came amongst the people and He saw that they were given to sinful words, and He did take the words away from them, so that they might speak but neither read nor write, leaving but one who might still have that gift. The Wordslinger.'

'And that's you?'

Manco nodded. 'It passes down through my family. My mother, and her father before her. But I have no mate, and no children, so I am the last.'

The Doctor nodded. Manco's last words had struck a chord inside him, and he looked across the dungeon to his fellow prisoner with sympathy.

'Tell me about these *Sittuun*,' he said. 'You said there were grey people from the stars?'

'Yes.' Manco replied. 'The Sittuun came here, to speak with Django. They said the star would hit this world and destroy it, and that there were other worlds, with other people, far away from here. They said the pieces of this world would be scattered out into the night, and that if just one of them were to hit another world, that it would kill *millions*.'

'And is that why they were here? The Sittuun?'

Manco nodded. 'They have a bomb,' he said. 'A bomb that could destroy the whole world, before the star comes. A bomb that would save all those millions...'

'And what happened to them? The Sittuun who came here?'

'Django said they were heretics,' Manco replied, his voice quiet and sombre. 'And he killed them for it.'

From the other side of the dungeon they heard the metallic wheezing of the main gate being opened, and Manco shrank away into one corner of his cell, cowering like an injured animal. It was Tuco, and he was followed by three more humans, each of them brandishing spears and pikes. They ignored Manco altogether, and stood before the Doctor.

'Django will see you now,' said Tuco, grinning devilishly. 'And Django isn't happy.'

Chapter
6

Captain Jamal stared at the outer casing of the Nanobomb. It was a cylindrical drum, almost a metre in length and half that in diameter. It was one of a kind; there was no bomb more powerful in the known universe. Deep inside its core there were a billion Nanites, microscopic robots with one function alone.

The bomb was designed to disperse the nanites over a radius of almost five hundred kilometres, a wide enough blast to cover the Gyre. The explosion itself, if it could be called that, would last just one-fifth of a second, with some of the Nanites travelling at over a thousand times the speed of sound to reach their destination. Once they had been dispersed, the Nanites would devour everything within the blast radius, whether it be animal, mineral or vegetable. Within four and a half seconds, an object with the size and mass of the Gyre, and everything on it, would be obliterated; a vague grey mist of disconnected atoms floating in the black void of space.

The Captain couldn't look at the bomb without feeling a tremendous sense of both awe and trepidation. Awe because of its immense power, and trepidation because he knew that very soon he would have to detonate the bomb. Whether they had escaped the Gyre or not.

Without looking over his shoulder, he felt the presence of another person in the bomb chamber. He turned slowly to see that it was Slipstream.

'Say, Captain… We're just about ready for the off. Seems the girl is coming with me, and your two young lads. Hope you don't mind. Say! Is that it? Is that the Nanobomb?'

The Captain nodded silently.

'Well, isn't she a beaut? Saw one of these go off in the Straits of Copernicus once, you know. Took out a whole mountain range in the blinking of an eye. One minute they were there, the next… pffft! Like that. Gone. Anyway… Thought it best to let you know we'll be going soon. TTFN, as they say.'

With a wink and a smile, Slipstream left the bomb chamber, whistling a happy tune as he went.

*

His rifle still charging, Charlie sat on the edge of his bed and watched the glowing green bar creep its way slowly along the barrel. He had been alone for no more than ten minutes, and all that time he had waited for a knock, or a voice calling his name, so it was no surprise when it came.

'Baasim… Can I come in?' It was his father's voice, speaking in Sittuun.

'Yes.'

The door opened, and Captain Jamal entered the room. He looked angry.

'You're charging your rifle?'

Charlie nodded.

'Then you're still serious about joining this… *Slipstream*… and going to the human city?'

'Yes. Yes I am.'

Captain Jamal shook his head. 'This is insane,' he said. 'It's a suicide mission.'

'This is all a suicide mission, Dad,' said Charlie, getting to his feet. 'The last hundred days have been one long suicide mission. We've got no way of getting off this thing, so we can either wait for the comet to hit us, or we can set off the Nanobomb. Either way, we're dead. I'd rather meet my end knowing I'd *tried* to save someone, than just waiting for death.'

His father closed the door behind him and spoke in hushed tones. 'It doesn't *have* to be that way,' he said. 'Slipstream has a ship. A *working* ship.'

'Yes, and he's going to rescue the Doctor. So we're stuck here until he does.'

'Not necessarily.'

Charlie stepped away from his father and laughed nervously. What could he mean? He looked at him, trying to read his expression, but Captain Jamal remained stoic.

'You don't mean…?'

'Baasim… That ship is in fine working order. When Slipstream and the human girl have gone, we can fly out of here.'

Charlie started shaking his head. 'No,' he said. 'No, Dad… I can't believe you'd even *suggest* that…'

'Why not?' asked the Captain. 'The clock is ticking, son. Need I remind you that our *world* is one of those at risk if Schuler-Khan hits the Gyre? A billion Sittuun men, women and children. Our *family* is at risk. Our *home*. Three human lives for a billion of your own kind?'

Charlie fell back onto his bed and put his head in his hands. He knew that his father was, in his own way, right, but he still felt responsible for Amy and the Doctor. If they had only given them the chance, when they had met in the valley, none of this would have happened. Amy and the Doctor might have been able to help them, as Amy said.

'It's not just three human lives, though, Dad,' he said at last. 'What about those in the human city?'

Captain Jamal laughed incredulously. 'Those *savages*?' he said. 'Have you forgotten that those... those *monsters* have killed six of our crew? And what is it with you and these *humans* anyway? I knew we shouldn't have sent you to the Lux Academy. You came back, and everything about you had changed. Calling yourself *Charlie*... What kind of a name is Charlie?'

Charlie laughed derisively. 'How many times do we have to have this discussion, Dad? And last time I checked, *Jamal* was hardly a Sittuun name...'

'Don't talk to me like that, Baasim. I may be your father, but I'm also your commanding officer, and I am *ordering* you to stay on this ship. Is that understood?'

Charlie looked up at his father with an insolent glower, but he knew it was no use. His father wouldn't take no for an answer, and besides, before he had the chance to argue any further, there was another knock at the door.

'Yes?' said Charlie.

The door opened just a little. It was Amy.

'I'm sorry... But Dirk says we have to go. Now.'

Charlie looked from Amy to his father, and then back again.

'I'm not coming,' he said.

Amy's face became drawn, an expression of disappointment. She sighed.

'Really? But—'

'I *can't*,' said Charlie. 'I'm sorry.'

'Right. OK. Well... I'm going. Thanks for...' She paused, rolling her eyes. 'I don't know... The *soup*?'

Then she turned her back and walked away. Charlie could sense her anger. He had been around humans enough to know when they weren't happy.

'Amy!' he cried out. He made to follow her but, before he could leave the room, his father had grasped him by the arm.

'You are staying on this ship,' the Captain snapped. 'Don't think I wouldn't go ahead with the plan if you didn't.'

'Ah, there you are, Miss Pond. Glad you could join us. We're just about ready for the off.'

Slipstream and Ahmed were in the loading bay, packing provisions onto the buggy. Amy nodded to each of them in turn, but said nothing. She just wanted to leave, to get out of there. Maybe they *could* rescue the Doctor, and then Slipstream could take them back to the TARDIS, and they could just leave. Another moment's hesitation would just be wasted time.

Ahmed looked past her, to where Charlie was now standing in the doorway.

'Come on, Charlie,' he said. 'We're going.'

'I'm not,' Charlie replied. 'I'm staying here.'

Ahmed frowned. He looked stung.

'What? But you said—'

'I know. But I can't. I just can't.'

Ahmed turned to Slipstream and then Amy. He looked at the buggy.

'Well, lad...' said Slipstream. 'What's it going to be then, eh? Are you coming with us, or are you staying here with your friend? That's the thing with these Sittuun, Miss Pond. No fear, or so they say. But it takes fear to be truly courageous...'

Ahmed's expression changed from one of disappointment to determination. He turned to Charlie.

'I'm going.'

Captain Jamal now entered the loading bay, but didn't speak. His eyes were fixed on his son with a stern glare.

'And we're taking Ella,' Ahmed added, patting the side of the buggy. 'If that's all right.'

Charlie nodded, but it was as if he couldn't bear to look at them, his gaze fixed on the ground. Amy caught his glance just once and shook her head, and Charlie looked away.

'Right-ho!' said Slipstream. 'All aboard. Looks like we're going.'

Ahmed climbed into the driving seat, then Slipstream sat beside him. Turning her back on Charlie, Amy mounted the back of the buggy, bracing herself against its tubular metal frame. As the engine revved into life, Charlie looked up at her one last time before they drove out, down a long ramp and out into the great, grey expanse of the Gyre.

Chapter

7

'You know, I've been frogmarched by quite a few people in my time, but you guys really have it down to a fine art. Did you know that?'

Neither Tuco nor the guards answered him.

The Doctor sighed. 'Funny word, isn't it? "Frogmarched", I mean. For one thing, frogs don't march, do they? Well... Earth frogs don't, anyway.'

Tuco glowered at him. 'What is a frog?' he snapped.

'Oh. Right,' said the Doctor. 'Green thing. Likes ponds.'

'You are not a frog.'

'No, Tuco... I wasn't saying that *I'm* a frog, I was saying that... Oh, never mind. I guess some of the more eccentric idioms of the English language have fallen by the wayside with you people.'

'Be quiet.'

They were dragging him along one of the subterranean tunnels beneath the human city, past gloomy alcoves in which cowering, bestial humans sat around flickering fires, gnawing at scraps of grisly-looking, overcooked meat.

They left the tunnel and passed through a large chamber, at the far end of which was a white sheet, suspended from the ceiling. A congregation of perhaps a hundred humans sat before the sheet, watching as the flickering image of a film was projected onto it.

There was no sound, only the images, and the Doctor noticed that it was a Western. A sheriff in a white hat hid behind a barrel, loading his pistol, while in the distance four gunslingers in black marched purposefully towards him along a dusty street. A human in long black robes stood next to the screen, and spoke in a loud, booming voice that echoed out across the chamber.

'And Wyturp, brother of Gobo, waited for the servants of the Bad, who had come to Oh-Kaykrall to destroy him.'

All too soon they had left the chamber and entered another tunnel.

'What was that?' asked the Doctor.

'That was the Chamber of Stories,' said Tuco.

'So you have electricity? And *films*? You have films? And *Wyturp* and *Oh Kaykrall*... Doesn't he mean *Wyatt* Earp and the *OK Corral*?'

Tuco shook his head and grunted. 'Do you know nothing, heathen?' he hissed. 'They are the stories. The stories of the Olden Ones, given to us by Gobo through his son Zasquez and passed down through generations.'

The Doctor thought about this for a moment, and then he laughed.

'Yes!' he said. 'Of course! El Paso! You've been watching *Westerns*. For *thousands* of years. And without the *sound* for most of it. No wonder you're getting the names all mixed up. Tell me, Tuco... The man back there. The one telling the story. He mentioned Gobo. Is Gobo actually *in* any of the films?'

Tuco scowled. 'Of course not!' he bellowed. 'Gobo never appears in the pictures. That is forbidden. The stories of the Olden Ones are about his sons, and his brothers, and the Bad, and the servants of the Bad.'

'Right,' said the Doctor. 'Of course.'

None of them had said a word since leaving the *Beagle XXI*, and they were nearing the far side of the desert of broken glass before Ahmed spoke.

'It's his father,' he said. 'Captain Jamal. He's the one who got him the job on the ship. He never approves of anything Charlie does.'

'Yes,' sneered Slipstream. 'Typical Sittuun behaviour, that. I've never known a species like them for red tape and high horses. Little wonder they've no time for gallantry. They're too busy crossing Ts and dotting Is.'

Ahmed glowered across at Slipstream and then returned his attention to the road ahead.

In the back of the buggy, Amy gazed up at the dark blue skies above the Gyre. There, directly above them, the comet, Schuler-Khan, was still visible. It looked larger now; near enough the same size in the night sky as the moon looked back on Earth.

Behind its shining orb there trailed a narrow mist of green and purple gas. It looked like a single, colourful and shimmering flame suspended in space. She turned to Ahmed, looking at him in the rear-view mirror.

'Why does everyone call him Charlie?' she asked. 'His Dad calls him *Baasim*.'

'Charlie's just his nickname,' replied Ahmed. 'He studied ancient Earth music at the Lux Academy over in Sol 1. Sorry… I mean *your* solar system. Got his name from some saxophone player he really liked. Same as Ella here…'

He drummed his hands on the steering wheel.

'Named *her* after a singer. If you ask me, Charlie's half human, he's spent that much time around them. It's a wonder he hasn't grown a nose and eyebrows. Ha ha…' He looked at Amy in the mirror. 'Sorry… That's not very politically correct, is it?'

Amy laughed. She wasn't sure why she should be offended by someone talking about noses and eyebrows. After all, the Sittuun were the weird ones for not having them. Weren't they?

When Ahmed noticed her laughing he smiled at her. 'You know something?' he said. 'For a human, you're all right.'

They had left the desert of broken glass and were now riding up and over one of the scrap mounds, heading back towards the valley where the TARDIS had landed. If only, Amy thought, the Doctor could have given her a driving lesson in that thing before they had come here. As it was, the console of the TARDIS was the most confusing thing she'd ever seen; so many dials and levers, buttons and bells. She wouldn't have known where to start.

'Say, Ahmed, old chap,' said Slipstream, as they drove on, past towering columns of scrap metal and the rusting remnants of long-forgotten spacecraft. 'I trust you know the way?'

Ahmed nodded. 'We went there once,' he said solemnly. 'Just the once.'

Slipstream gazed out from the buggy at the decaying vistas around them.

'I'd always wondered what this place would be

like,' he said, his voice sounding suddenly faraway and dreamy. 'Back when I was a boy.'

'You'd heard about it then?' asked Ahmed.

'Oh yes. There were many stories and legends about the Gyre. Many of them fanciful, of course. After all, nobody had set foot on this thing. Well… As far as we knew. That only seemed to lend it a greater air of mystery. It was a truly *new world*. A world of our own making. There was talk of a great treasure being here, somewhere…'

'Treasure?' asked Amy. 'What, like gold?'

Slipstream and Ahmed both laughed.

'What? What's so funny?'

'Ha ha… My dear girl. Gold? Gold's worthless. Were you brought up in the outer nebulae?'

'Why? I don't get it…'

'Voga and Midas Superior,' said Ahmed, sounding far less condescending than Slipstream. 'Gold planets. Midas Superior was solid gold from core to crust. Not much left of either of them now, of course…'

'Well of *course*,' said Amy, with a trace of sarcasm.

'No,' Slipstream continued. 'There may be plenty of gold here on the Gyre, but that isn't the treasure. Legend has it that the Gyre was the final resting place of the Mymon Key.'

Amy was pleased to notice that Ahmed looked as clueless as her at the mention of this name. At least she wasn't the only one.

'What's the Mymon Key?'

'Oh, I don't know,' said Slipstream. 'Probably nothing more than a folk story. A fairy tale. They say it was engineered on a distant world, out beyond Cassiopeia's Elbow. A device of unimaginable power. The owner of the Mymon Key could wield the greatest power in the universe.' He smiled and winked at Amy in the mirror. 'Still,' he said. 'Probably just a fairy tale, eh?'

They had entered a long, narrow gully between two vast and almost limitless piles of scrap, each rising up in sheer cliff faces to either side. With the nearest stars and planets, and the dim green glow of Schuler-Khan cut off, the world around them grew darker and the air a little colder. Amy braced herself against the cold and shuddered.

With no one in the buggy talking, she was able to just sit and think, and there were so many things to think about; too many things. She was reminded of that feeling when, after a long and heavy night out, it became clear there was no way home. No taxis at the ranks; the last bus having left several hours earlier. They were always rainy nights, those times when she and her friends would find themselves stranded. Cold and rainy, almost without exception, and home – warm home and a warm bed – always seemed so far away. She could almost laugh about it now. On those nights, home was never more than five or six miles, walking distance, if you were wearing sensible shoes, and yet they'd do anything rather than walk.

Now home was so far away she struggled to grasp the sheer scale of it, both in miles and years. Looking up into the canyon, at the thin, jagged splinter of dark blue sky above them, she saw just a handful of stars. Could any one of them have been Earth's sun? She wasn't sure. Astronomy had never been her strong point. Even so, she decided to pick one, and make that the Sun. It wouldn't make any difference if it wasn't. Just picking that single star and deciding it was home brought some degree of comfort; a comfort only dampened by the thought that even if it *were* the sun, and even if the Earth *was* still spinning around it, it might be an Earth 2,500 centuries after her time.

'Dirk,' said Amy, looking at his reflection in the mirror, 'what's Earth like?'

Slipstream laughed. 'Earth? Well, I've only been the once, Miss Pond. Y'see, I grew up on Titan.'

'But what's it like?'

Slipstream mulled this over for a moment, and grimaced. 'Far too many tourists,' he said bluntly.

It wasn't the answer Amy had been looking for. She wanted to hear stories about magnificent cities made of glass, or cruise ships that floated through the clouds. She wanted him to tell her about robot butlers, or floating cities.

Still, what else could he tell her? If she had learned one thing about the future, it was that it was nothing like people said it would be.

Chapter
8

Charlie sat alone in his quarters, looking at the rifle, now fully charged, that he would never use. He knew that elsewhere on the ship his father and Dr Heeva would be preparing the Nanobomb for detonation, and he felt something, a feeling or an emotion, that he didn't recognise. It was like an aching in his chest, a real and physical pain. It was a mood that hung over him like the darkest of rain clouds.

He thought about Amy and Ahmed, driving across the Gyre in Ella, his buggy, and he realised he would never see them again. He had known Ahmed almost five years. They were the same age, and had joined the crew of the *Beagle XXI* at the same time. There had been some animosity at first;

Ahmed taunting Charlie, saying he'd only got the job because of his father. Of course, this was true, in part, but soon enough they became friends. They had seen so much of the universe together; each experience new for both of them. Ahmed was not just his friend, he was the best of friends.

But something else was gnawing away at Charlie. Something he couldn't quite fathom. Everything about that day's events seemed so unlikely. They had been on the Gyre for more than a hundred days, and there had been no answer to any of their distress calls. The Gyre was so remote that years and decades could pass without another ship passing it. And yet, in a single day, they had been joined by not one but two separate parties.

Amy, Charlie had decided, was trustworthy. His years at a university populated largely by humans had given him some understanding of their ways and customs. He knew when humans were lying and when they were telling the truth, most of the time. No, she was fine, and if she trusted the Doctor, then maybe he was fine too.

Which just left Slipstream.

On and on they drove through the dark gully. Biting winds that chilled her to the bone came sweeping through its gloomy, zigzagging corridor. In what little light there was, Amy saw long-forgotten and discarded relics on the side of the path: emptied containers, shattered belongings. She saw a plastic doll pinned to the ground by an old oil drum, its hollow eye sockets gazing up at the dark sky, and it made her sad. Sad because maybe its owner had died here, or maybe it had been lost or thrown away.

At last they left the gully and reached the precipice of a vast canyon, across which there lay a wide metal pipe. Ahmed brought the buggy to a halt, the engine still purring away.

'OK,' he said. 'This is where we have to be careful.'

Slipstream looked out across the canyon, squinting his eyes and toying with the ends of his moustache.

'Well… At least there's a bridge.'

'Except it's *not* a bridge,' said Ahmed. 'It's a pipe. As in, it's *round*. You ever tried steering a buggy on something that's *round*?'

'Nonsense!' Slipstream snorted. 'Just keep her straight, and drive on into those rushes yonder.'

He pointed across the gorge to where a forest of what looked like tall black reeds were swaying in the wind.

'And that's the other thing,' said Ahmed. 'That's where the Sollogs live.'

Slipstream snapped his head in Ahmed's direction, his eyebrows bunching together.

'Sollogs? What in the devil's name is a *Sollog*?'

Ahmed looked from Slipstream to Amy. He looked worried. No, *more* than worried. He looked genuinely terrified.

'They're... they're like slugs,' he said. 'Giant slugs.'

Slipstream laughed.

'My dear chap... It'll take more than a few pesky molluscs to get Dirk Slipstream's knickers in a twist. Drive on.'

Ahmed revved the engine again, and took the buggy closer to the edge of the canyon.

'Is there another way?' asked Amy. 'Some other way around that doesn't involve crossing a ridiculously deep canyon and ending up in a swamp filled with giant slugs?'

Ahmed shook his head.

'Like I said, Ahmed, drive on,' said Slipstream. 'There's a good chap.'

Taking a deep breath and flexing his smooth, grey fingers around the steering wheel, Ahmed started driving again. They were on the pipe, now, inching their way forward. The giant wheels of the buggy grumbled against the thick metal, flecks and shards of rust falling away and tumbling down into the darkness like orange snowflakes. Each time they hit a slimy, gnarled length of vine the buggy bounced. Amy peered over the side and felt giddy with vertigo.

'Tad faster, if you would...' said Slipstream.

Ahmed glanced over at him with a resentful sneer, but then snapped his gaze back to the road ahead, if it could be called a road. To either side of them it curved around before falling away altogether. If they over-steered just a little to the left or right they could lose their grip on the pipe, and be sent tumbling down into the bottomless ravine. Amy hadn't breathed in or out in an age.

They were halfway across the bridge when Amy heard it.

Something was tapping on the metal beneath them, like a metallic Morse code.

'Can you hear that?' she whispered.

'Hear what?' asked Slipstream. He sat with one arm slung nonchalantly over the side of the buggy, as if he hadn't a care in the world.

'That tapping,' said Amy. 'Listen.'

'I can't hear anything, Miss Pond. It's your mind... playing tricks with you. That's the thing with ladies, Ahmed, old chap. They *do* have a frightful tendency to let their imaginations get the better of them.'

'I'm not *imagining* it!' snapped Amy. 'Listen.'

The buggy drove on another two metres, its passengers silent, and then she heard it again.

'Yeah... I heard that,' said Ahmed.

'Oh, don't *you* start,' Slipstream sneered. 'There's nothing *there*. Just drive on. That damned comet will have smashed us into atoms by the time we get to the other side, at the rate we're going.'

There was another tap, this one louder than the last, and this time they all heard it.

'It's probably *nothing*. Just a lot of old rust rattling around inside the pi—'

Before Slipstream could finish his sentence they saw it. The Sollog. It crawled up from the side of the pipe with spider-like movements, its slimy trunk squirming between eight gangling, bony limbs. For a moment it just stood there, blocking their path, but then its eyes lifted up on gelatinous stalks, and it stared right at them. Then it hissed.

Slipstream moved fast. Drawing his pistol from its holster, he aimed and fired at the creature, a pulse of green light flashing towards it. The Sollog moved even faster, and dived out of the way, its sucker-like feet clinging to the pipe.

'Damn and blast!' shouted Slipstream.

He took aim and fired again, missing the Sollog but hitting the side of the pipe, splitting it wide open in a cloud of powdered rust. Slipstream turned to Ahmed, his face contorting with rage.

'Drive!' he yelled. 'Damn you, drive!'

The Sollog hissed at them again and charged at the buggy, ramming into it with shocking force. As Ahmed slammed his foot into the accelerator the back end of the vehicle swerved wildly to the left, one of its wheels slipping down into the gaping hole left by Slipstream's second shot.

The buggy shook violently, and Ahmed was thrown from the driver's seat and onto the pipe. He landed on his side and slid down, further away from the buggy, until he was hanging over the gorge, holding on to the edge of the blast hole by his fingertips.

'No!' Amy screamed, reaching out for him, but it was no use. He was too far away.

Slipstream had already climbed into the driver's seat. He hit the accelerator, and the buggy's wheels spun and howled beneath them.

'What are you *doing*?' cried Amy. 'We have to help him!'

But Slipstream wasn't listening to her. He drove on along the pipe, the buggy swerving from side to side. With a sudden gasp, Amy climbed up onto the buggy's frame, looking back to where Ahmed was still hanging from the side of the pipe. Even though the Sollog was still giving chase, scuttling after them with its eight legs a blur of motion, she prepared to jump, closing her eyes, and holding her breath.

'Don't even think about it, Miss Pond,' said Slipstream. With one hand bracing the steering wheel, he had turned around and had his pistol aimed straight for her. 'Get back where you were.'

Terrified, Amy sat back down, and Slipstream fired another shot at the Sollog. This time the creature was not so lucky, and it burst in a shower of dark green gunk. The blast from the pistol slammed straight into the pipe, tearing open another gaping, smouldering wound. Beneath them, the pipe groaned; a metallic howl that echoed down into the canyon. It shuddered and shook, and slowly they felt it beginning to sag.

Fissures appeared around the second crater left by Slipstream's gun, spreading wider. The pipe was splitting in two.

'No!' said Amy, more to herself than Slipstream. 'No… I've got to help him.'

She closed her eyes again. This was it. She could stay in the buggy, or she could jump out. Slipstream was facing forward again, his eyes focused on the other side of the gorge. This was her chance.

Taking a deep breath she stood and she jumped. The split second before she landed seemed stretched out into an eternity, when all around her became silent, and in that boundless moment she thought about home, and the Doctor, and the dress she might never wear.

She landed on her side with a heavy thump, rolling twice before coming to a stop, and she spread her arms and legs as quickly as she could and held on to the pipe, fearing it might dip once more. Then, when she had gathered herself, she stood and began running back to where Ahmed was still clinging to the gaping hole by his fingertips.

'It's OK!' she shouted. 'I'm coming!'

She was halfway to him when the pipe groaned again, and now she heard a monstrous crunch as it began to buckle and break. Again, the world slowed down, and she looked back to see Slipstream reach the far side of the canyon, the buggy screeching to a halt. She turned once more to Ahmed, and saw his expression of fear.

Then the pipe broke.

Amy breathed in as the ground beneath her fell away. Looking down, she saw Ahmed, falling from the pipe, his mouth open in a scream she couldn't hear, before he was swallowed by the darkness.

She turned, and realised she was floating, or rather *falling*, and she reached out with both hands, grasping at the pipe that had, until seconds ago, been beneath her feet. Her fingers clawed at nothing but its rusty shell until, and not too soon, they found a length of vine, and she clutched at it and held on to it for dear life.

The pipe swung down and slammed into the face of the gorge with a bellowing clang, but still she held on. Then there was silence.

Amy looked up the cliff face to its edge.

'Help!' she screamed. 'Please! Help me!'

After several long and agonising seconds, Dirk Slipstream appeared, leaning over the precipice.

'Help me!' Amy cried once more.

'Oh dear,' said Slipstream. 'Terribly sorry, Miss Pond. I'm afraid this is where we part company.

You see… I've got a rather pressing matter to attend to.'

'What?' Amy snapped. 'What are you talking about?'

'It's a shame, really. Always looks good, rescuing girls. Anyway… So long.'

He offered her a final, mocking wave of the hand before he vanished, and Amy heard the revving of the buggy's engine. After a few seconds there was silence once more.

Amy clutched at the vine, and though a part of her was screaming and telling her not to, she looked down. The black and bottomless depths of the canyon stretched out beneath her, and looked for just that moment like a vast, malevolent grin.

Chapter
9

From the tunnel, they climbed a spiral staircase that corkscrewed its way up a dank and gloomy tower, until eventually they came to another chamber, even larger than the last. This one was dimly lit with flickering torches and fluorescent strips that blinked on and off. The chamber's ceiling was supported by columns made from old oil drums, and the central knave was lined with grisly, humanoid statues, cobbled together from shreds of scrap metal.

At the far end of the aisle a large metal panel bearing the image of Gobo, the cartoon clown, was riveted to the wall. The blinking of the fluorescent strips and the flickering of the torches cast twisted, monstrous shadows onto the clown's face. Beneath the image was a raised platform, on which sat a large iron throne.

When they had reached the far end of the knave, the guards dropped the Doctor to the ground, and he landed with a heavy thud.

'Ow!' wheezed the Doctor. 'Easy...'

He heard a drum roll from beyond the chamber, a slow and funereal pounding that grew louder and louder. Tuco had climbed onto the platform's edge, and he held up his staff, his menacing green eyes fixed on the chamber's ceiling.

'In the beginning,' he bellowed, 'was the dark blue night and the silence and the empty and the none. And into this came Gobo. Chosen is he who rules this Earth. Chosen is Django the Wise, son of Rojo the Victorious, of the line of Zasquez. All hail Django!'

The guards around the Doctor echoed Tuco's words, and then, from the platform's side, another human entered the chamber. He was tall in stature, and long-limbed, his straggly brown hair reaching down to his shoulders, his face half hidden with a mottled birds nest of a beard. His eyes were wide, the pupils so large they reduced his irises to nothing, making each eye appear as black as obsidian. He gazed down at the Doctor with an almost casual indifference and sat on his throne.

For a moment there was near-silence, the only sound in the chamber the buzzing of the fluorescent strips and the gentle but ominous lapping of the torch flames. When Django breathed it was with a coarse, diseased rattle, like the sound of bare branches creaking in a storm.

'Who is this?' he growled, his deep voice echoing through the chamber.

'He is a heretic,' said Tuco. 'Our men found him beyond the canyon, in the valleys. He was with the Sittuun.'

The Doctor was now standing again, brushing the dirt from his jacket and straightening his bow tie. 'I take it you're Django,' he said.

Django stared at him, his manic eyes peering out through the strands of dirty hair that formed a thin veil across his face. 'Yes. I am Django. And who are you?'

'I'm the Doctor.'

Django smiled, a graveyard grin of tombstone teeth. 'And why are you here?'

'Well... I'm *here* because your people threw a rope net over my head, tied my hands together, dragged me here and then threw me in a cell.'

'Do not joke, *Doctor*... It won't save your life.'

'Right...' said the Doctor, hesitantly. 'OK... I didn't realise this was a life-and-death situation. Well, OK... Maybe the thought *had* crossed my mind. But nobody had mentioned it...'

Django grunted, looking across at Tuco. 'You say he's a heretic?'

Tuco nodded. 'Yes, Master. He spoke about a *ship*. He said this is not Earth. He claims knowledge of the times before the Earth. Before even Gobo.'

Django gasped, sitting back in his throne and looking at the Doctor with evident disgust.

'What could you know of the times before the Earth, you insolent swine?'

The Doctor paused for a moment. Should he speak again? He'd tried arguing his point with people like this, of many different species, on many different occasions, and it rarely got him anywhere. Still, what else could he do? He took a deep breath.

'I know who you are,' he said. 'I know *what* you are. I *think* I know what this... this *world*... this place you call Earth... I think I know what it is. Why it's here.'

'Impossible,' Django sneered. 'You can know nothing of these things. They are the knowledge of Gobo.'

'OK,' said the Doctor. 'What about just now? You called me a swine. Do you even *know* what a swine is? Do you *have* pigs here?'

Django frowned, turning to Tuco. 'Tuco,' he said. 'What are "pigs"?'

Tuco shrugged.

'See!' said the Doctor. 'You're using words and you don't even know what they mean. Words that got passed down, generation after generation, and lost all their meaning. Listen, Django… *mate*… we can carry on talking about heresy and the Story of Earth and Gobo the Great and Terrible until the cows come home, even if you don't *have* any cows, but you *need* to know… Something very bad is about to happen to this place.'

Django smiled again, brushing some of the hair from his face, and he leaned forward in his throne.

'Oh yes, Doctor?' he said. 'And what is this "something bad"?'

'The star,' said the Doctor. 'The Star with the Green Tail, or whatever it is you choose to call it… The one that's in the sky right now? That star is a *comet*. It's called Schuler-Khan. It is a ball of rock and ice about five hundred metres in diameter, and it is heading straight for us. By my calculations, it will hit this world in less than a day's time, and it will kill everyone and everything here. You included.'

Django sat back once more. He smiled, and then he clapped his hands together with glee.

'Ha! Doctor… This is what you have to tell us? *This* is the heresy for which you will risk your life? Do you think we have not been told these lies before?'

The Doctor frowned. 'I'm sorry… What do you mean?'

'The Sittuun. The grey people from the sky. Messengers of the Bad. They came here and they

101

told us the same. And do you know what I said to them?'

'No.'

'I said to them, "Prove it." I said, "If what you tell us is true – that we are all from some other place, and that this star is coming to destroy us – prove it." And they couldn't. They showed me images, pictures on a screen, and they spoke of numbers, but these things prove nothing. We have been here for thousands of years. Our stories are as old as the sky. How could they *not* be true? So I say to you, Doctor… If what *you* are saying is true… Prove it.'

'What? *Now*?'

'Yes, Doctor. Here and now, prove that we are from this other place.'

'Well… If you would let me into your tower, maybe I could find–'

'Nobody goes into the tower.'

'Well, then… how am I supposed to pro–'

'Prove it here. And now.'

'But… that's just… Django, that's not possible. I can't prove it *here* and *now*, but if you just gave me the chance to–'

'Do you see?' said Django, grinning at Tuco and the other humans gathered in the chamber. 'See how the lies of the Bad are exposed! You heard him! You heard him say the words: "*I can't prove it.*" He *can't* prove it. You can't prove it, *Doctor*, and neither could the Sittuun. They told us they had come to destroy the Earth. To save it, they said. Yes... Save it, from the star they call "comet".'

'And they were right!' the Doctor shouted, allowing his frustration to show for the first time. 'They were telling you the *truth*, Django. They were trying to *help* you.'

Django shook his head, still smiling. 'No, Doctor. They weren't. And we killed them for their lies. The star is not "comet". These are the lies of the Bad. The star is Gobo.'

'What? *What*? Are you out of your mind?'

'The star is Gobo, Doctor. The star is here to take us from the Earth, to the land of El Paso.'

The Doctor sighed and closed his eyes, his shoulders slumping. He looked down at the ground. What could he do? There were hundreds, maybe thousands of humans living in the city. Thousands of lives, and no matter how ignorant or savage they were, no matter how badly they had treated him, he couldn't bring himself to let those lives be extinguished because of one man's insanity.

'Please,' he said. 'Django, I am *begging* you... You have to listen to me. I have a ship... It's in the valley where your men found me. It can take you anywhere. There must be children here. At least let me save *them*. I can take them to another planet, somewhere *safe*. Or... or...'

He pulled at his hair, thoughts racing through

his mind at such a rate he struggled to keep up with them.

'Maybe I could… maybe there's some way we could use the TARDIS to…'

'They *will* be saved, Doctor,' said Django, rising from his throne and glaring down at him. 'When Gobo has come, they *will* be saved.'

'No!' the Doctor cried. 'They will be killed. *You* will be killed. All of you.'

Django turned to Tuco. 'He is a heretic,' he growled. 'The penalty for heresy is death. Take him to Lake Mono.'

With a dismissive gesture of one hand, Django walked out of his throne room, a coterie of guards following closely behind. From the platform Tuco looked down at the Doctor and laughed.

'Ha ha…' he said tauntingly. 'No need to worry about "comet" now, Doctor. You are going to Lake Mono.'

The Doctor chewed his lip and gazed up at Tuco with a grimace.

'And I'm guessing that's not a good thing…'

Tuco shook his head, still smirking maliciously.

'Oh no,' he cackled. 'Mono is a lake of acid, in which nothing can survive. Guards… Take him away.'

Chapter
10

So this is it, thought Amy. *I'm going to die here in this horrible place, and nobody will know. Everyone back home will just think I've run off to somewhere far away and exotic, like Thailand or South America, and the worst thing is, I won't be anywhere. Not for them. I won't be anywhere for another two hundred and fifty thousand years. I'll just be gone. Vanished.*

Her entire body ached, a throbbing pain that grew more intense with every passing second. She had managed to wrap some of the vines around her arms and legs, but they were slippery with slime, and she wasn't sure how much longer she could hold on, or how much longer the vines would hold. All she knew was that she didn't want to let go.

Looking up she saw the comet, Schuler-Khan.

It appeared even larger now than the last time she had looked at it.

Maybe, she thought, *if I'm lucky, that thing will hit this place before I fall.*

The thought made her shudder. Would that *really* be preferable? She hated thinking that way, but could see no other way out of this. What if she let go, and the canyon was even deeper than she could imagine? Deeper than any canyon on Earth? What if it was almost *literally* bottomless. She could fall for hours, days maybe. Her hands gripped the vine a little tighter than before, and another spasm of pain shot through her muscles.

But what was that? She could hear something, from above the canyon's gaping, crooked maw. A heavy whirring. Was it the buggy? No, it was a different sound, almost like a helicopter. Daring to open her eyes once more, she looked up. The sound was getting louder.

She looked across to the far side of the canyon and saw something emerging from above the crest of a jagged plateau. It looked almost like a spaceship of some sort, but it was smaller, perhaps no bigger than the buggy. The craft rose up high above the narrow, twisting gully through which they had travelled, and then dipped down towards the canyon, sweeping from side to side like a mechanical bumblebee. Only as it drew closer could Amy see the pilot in its cockpit.

It was Charlie.

The tiny flying craft came down into the canyon, its small body kept aloft by twin blades. The canopy swung open on hinges, and Charlie leaned out.

'Amy!' he shouted. 'I'm going to come in close, but I'll need you to jump. Can you do that?'

Though she knew she shouldn't, Amy looked down into the abyss once more and felt a lurching sensation in her stomach. She looked up at Charlie and nodded.

'Right… OK…' said Charlie.

With the canopy still open, he pulled the joystick just a fraction of an inch. The flying craft drew closer, turning in mid air so that it was now only a few metres away. Amy could feel the downdraft of wind from its rotors. Her arms and legs were in agony now, and her hands were numb. Charlie was reaching for her from the cockpit, but the distance between them could have been miles as far as she was concerned.

'OK, this is as close as I can get,' said Charlie. 'You *have* to jump. On the count of three. OK? One…'

Amy closed her eyes and took a deep breath.

'Two…'

She opened them again and nodded.

'Three!'

Amy jumped, and for just a fraction of a second she was neither clinging to the pipe nor safe inside the cockpit, but floating, floating above the black void of the canyon. A single thought raced through her mind, but it was a thought built on so many others.

I can't believe this is actually happening.

Just seven words, in all, but each one loaded with meaning. She couldn't believe she had jumped. She couldn't believe she was jumping onto some kind of spacecraft. She couldn't believe she was jumping onto some kind of spacecraft on an alien world light years from Earth, at some point in the very distant future.

That was what she was *really* thinking, when she thought those seven words and so, when she landed in Charlie's arms, and he held on to her tight, her first instinct was to laugh. Charlie closed the canopy and steered them up out of the canyon's jaws, and they were flying now over the swamp of swaying plastic tubes. Looking down, Amy saw Sollogs, perhaps hundreds of them, scuttling through the swamp. It was then that she started to cry.

Charlie brought them down a little way past the swamp, on the edge of the great salt flats.

'We can't fly much further, or we'll be spotted,' he said.

The cockpit was cramped with the two of them, its confines clearly designed for just a single pilot and no passengers, but Amy didn't mind. It felt like she had spent an eternity clinging to that pipe, staring down into an infinite space. The experience had left her far from claustrophobic.

'What happened?' asked Charlie. 'Where are Slipstream and Ahmed?'

Amy wiped the tears from her eyes.

'Ahmed's dead,' she said. 'And Slipstream... Slipstream just left us there.'

'I'm not surprised,' he said. 'There's a *lot* Slipstream didn't tell us.'

Charlie looked out through the window at the glittering white desert before them and closed his eyes.

'Ahmed's dead?' he asked.

'Yes. I'm sorry.'

Charlie took a deep breath and then sighed.

'We have to go back,' he said. 'My father is setting off the Nanobomb. He's going to take Slipstream's ship.'

'What? But we can't... The Doctor...'

Charlie hunched over in the pilot's seat with his head in his hands. 'I knew you were going to say that.'

'Well I'm not going without him. He's my only way home. No... It's more than that, actually. He's my *friend*. I'm not leaving him here.'

Charlie sighed. 'OK. Look... The Nanobomb's detonation sequence lasts one hour. It's designed to allow you time to get to a safe distance. If we go *now*, we might just have time to go to the human city and get him.'

'Really?'

Charlie nodded, but now he was looking back across the salt flats at the towering black hulk on the horizon. Amy followed his gaze and saw the flickering orange lights in the watchtowers.

'Only trouble is,' said Charlie, 'we have to find a way in. But I think I have an idea…'

Chapter
11

Without a doubt, the Gyre was the ugliest world he had ever visited. He had seen the manure oceans of Caranexos and the living, breathing, continent of Mrag on Hellion D, but nothing compared to this.

Everything about it was aesthetically distasteful. The landscape was a barren wasteland of twisted metal and spilled chemicals. The plant life consisted largely of spiky green shrubs and things with thorns. And as for the wildlife…

Dirk Slipstream's once immaculate silver spacesuit was now soiled, from his collar down to his ankles, with the viscous remains of almost every Sollog he had vanquished in the swamp. Those disgusting creatures had *insisted* on bursting almost every time he shot them, showering him in a green slime with the consistency of tar. Still, once he had killed the first six, the others had learned their lesson and run away.

The buggy had taken quite a beating, passing through the swamp. The towering plastic tubes had played havoc with its chassis, and one of the rear wheels had been punctured. Still, it was in good enough condition to get him across the salt plain, and that was what mattered.

The only problem was, he hadn't quite figured out a way to get back when he was finished, but he cast this moment's doubt to the back of his mind. Dirk Slipstream always found a way. After all, he'd found a way out of Volag-Noc after six years of imprisonment there, and the judge at his trial had told him it was inescapable. He had found a way to steal the *Golden Bough* from its rightful owner. He had found his way to the Gyre with only hours to spare.

Yes. Dirk Slipstream would find a way.

As the buggy neared the human city, Slipstream heard the sound of drums and a fanfare of horns. He drove on until he had reached the gates, and then he climbed out. A human guard stood in one of the watchtowers, staring down at him.

'Good afternoon!' said Slipstream. 'I don't suppose you could be a gent and open up these gates for me, what?'

The guard grunted something, and then turned

away, speaking to somebody on the other side of the outer wall. Seconds later the gates began to open, and a small army of guards spilled out onto the salt flat, all of them brandishing weapons. A handful of them set about attacking the buggy with their cudgels and blades, slashing at its tyres and denting its body, and one of them grabbed Slipstream and put a knife to his throat.

'Steady on, chaps,' Slipstream laughed. 'Not much of a welcoming committee, I must say. I suppose the phrase I'm looking for is "Take me to your leader".'

'So... The *Beagle XXI*. Your ship...'

'Yes?'

'Is that a *Sittuun* ship?'

Charlie turned to Amy, frowning. 'What do you mean?'

'Well... Was it made by the Sittuun? On your planet? It's just the name "Beagle". It's not Arabic like your names. It's an English word.'

They were still walking across the salt flat. They had been walking for what felt like an age, and the human city didn't seem any nearer.

'It's a human ship,' said Charlie. 'And it's European.'

'Right. OK. So do you guys work with humans a lot, then? When you're not stuck here, I mean.'

'Yes,' said Charlie. 'Our company, IEA is a

multi-world organisation, but right now it's mostly human and Sittuun.'

'Right. And you went to a university near Earth, yeah?'

'Ye-es. And?'

'Well… If you *work* with humans, and you went to university with lots of humans, what I don't get is why your Dad, and the others… why they have this big problem with humans.'

Charlie sighed. 'I thought we'd been through this.'

'Yeah, but it can't just be because we're superstitious and a bit, well, *warmongery*. I mean… Is that all it is?'

Charlie laughed softly. 'And "warmongery" isn't enough?' he said. 'No. For what it's worth, I don't think it's just that. But that's just my opinion.'

'So what *do* you think it is? If it's not just all the ghost stories and warmongering?'

'Earlier on, when I was telling you why we're called Sittuun, why we have Earth names, I told you we were first *encountered* by that Syrian crew, yes?'

'Yeah. I remember that bit.'

'Well… Think about it. That's when we were first *encountered*. By an *Earth* crew who had travelled through a wormhole using *Earth* technology. Humans were the first aliens we ever encountered.'

Amy thought about this for a moment. They were both still walking, flakes of salt still crunching with every footfall. Then it came to her.

'You mean you guys had never been into space?'

Charlie nodded.

'So,' Amy said, smiling now, 'you mean to say that humans were all, you know, spaceships and wormholes, and you guys were really primitive?'

'Er... we prefer the word *developing*.'

'But... why? Why weren't you travelling into space? I mean... You guys seem really intelligent. *Way* more intelligent than most of the humans I know. And you don't have any of the weird superstitions or... or... hang-ups that we have. My friend's grandmother still thinks you can tell somebody's future by looking at *tea leaves*. And you're telling me we're more *advanced* than *you*?'

Charlie shrugged. 'You know what I think?' he said. 'A part of me thinks it was your superstitions and your myths that got you there in the first place. We had nothing like that. We had our science and our history, but we didn't ask too many questions. We had no sense of *mystery*. On Earth you were making up stories about the stars and the planets hundreds, no *thousands* of years before you went there. And I think that made you want to go even more. This mad drive to answer all the questions, and then ask yourselves some more. The Sittuun don't like questions we can't answer right away.'

He stopped walking, and looked out towards the human city, shielding his eyes from the light of the comet, which seemed to grow brighter with every passing minute.

'I can see Ella,' he said. 'She's parked at the gates. And they've trashed her. Typical. Right... Do you remember the plan?'

Amy took a deep breath and let it out slowly. 'Yeah. I think so.'

'OK. Show me.'

Amy rolled her eyes, and then adopted a hunchbacked stance, twisting her face into a bestial frown. 'I have a prisoner,' she grunted.

Charlie laughed and shook his head. 'OK. That was a bit much,' he said. 'Do it again, only this time try and make it a little bit less "impression-of-a-caveman".'

Tutting under her breath, Amy adopted the stance again. 'I have a prisoner,' she said.

This time Charlie nodded. 'Yeah,' he said. 'Much better.'

In the throne room, Tuco stood on the raised platform and held his staff aloft.

'In the beginning was the dark blue night and the silence and the empty and the none. And into this came Gobo. Chosen is he who rules this Earth. Chosen is—'

'Yes yes yes. Get *on* with it,' said Dirk Slipstream. 'I haven't got all day.'

Tuco scowled at him. 'All hail Django!' he snarled, bringing down his staff with a triumphant thump.

Slipstream smiled knowingly, rubbing the palms of his hands together as if he were awaiting a prize.

Seconds later, Django entered the room followed by his guards. He climbed up onto the platform, and sat on his throne, looking down at Slipstream with an air of wild-eyed curiosity, as if caught in the middle of some mind-bending trance.

'Who *are* you?' he croaked. 'Who *sent* you?'

'Oh, nobody sent me old chap. This is more of a solo venture. You see, I believe I have information you fellas may find interesting.'

Django looked at Tuco, raising one eyebrow, and Tuco shrugged in return. Django's lunatic gaze returned to Slipstream.

'Yes? And what is this information?'

Slipstream smiled, his snow-white teeth twinkling in the dim glow of the torches.

'The Sittuun hideout. I know where they are. I know where their *bomb* is kept. You know about their bomb, don't you?'

'The bomb is the work of the Bad!' Django roared. 'They wish to destroy the Earth.'

Slipstream cleared his throat, trying not to

laugh. 'Yes. Well, quite. And I know where it is.'

'Tell me!'

'Easy, old boy. You see... There's something you can do for me in return.'

A deathly silence fell over the room and Django sat back on his throne, scratching at his straggly beard with long, bony fingers. His breathing grew heavy, a wheezing death rattle, and his lips curled back from his crooked, ashen teeth.

'What is it you want?' he asked.

'I want to go into your tower,' said Slipstream. 'This tower with... whatsisname... *Gobo* on the side of it.'

'Why?'

'Well, old chap... Just so happens there's something I want in there. It's nothing of interest to you, but it's very valuable to me.'

Django's expression darkened. 'Nobody goes into the tower,' he said. 'Nobody.'

'Ah, but then of course I *do* know where the Sittuun are hiding. Don't I? I thought maybe, on this occasion, you could make an exception.'

Tuco glanced anxiously from Slipstream to Django. He hunched himself over at the side of the throne and whispered into Django's ear:

'Master... He may be right. We *need* to find the Sittuun. Gobo grows greater by the day; his light gets ever brighter. If they explode the bomb... boom! What then?'

Slowly, Django began to nod. 'Yes,' he said. 'Yes... Maybe he is right.' He turned to Slipstream. 'Very well. You may go into the tower.'

Slipstream beamed. 'Ah, marvellous. I knew you'd see sense. Now... I'll need two things. First, a guide. Is there anyone who knows their way around the ship... I mean, the tower?'

Django and Tuco looked to one another. Tuco nodded, as if he understood some unspoken sentiment.

'There is one,' he said. 'The Wordslinger, Manco... the heretic. He has been into the tower.'

'Jolly good. I'll take him.'

'But he is our pris—'

'I won't hear a word of it. That tower of yours is a quarter of a mile tall. I'll need a guide, so I'm taking Manco...'

Tuco looked at Django, who gave his consent with a dismissive gesture of the hand.

'And this other thing?' Tuco asked. 'What is this other thing you need?'

They had left the city on its far side, behind the great towering hulk of the Gobocorp ship. Looking out into the distance, the Doctor saw another seemingly endless landscape of jagged and misshapen metal; mountains of debris, and valleys and canyons etched out of refuse.

'Tell me something, Sancho,' he said to his

guard. 'Your city... and your tower... is it by any chance the *centre* of the world?'

Sancho looked at him with a quizzical frown. 'Hmm?'

'Your tower. Is it slap bang, right in the middle of the world? Dead centre? Like a bulls-eye?'

Sancho shrugged. 'S'ppose so.'

'Right. I... see. Interesting.'

They took him out across a vast plain of copper that had turned green with rust; a single concave sheet of metal perhaps half a mile across that may have looked, from some distance, like a pasture, until they came at last to the lake's edge. The lake itself was immense, a bubbling cauldron of dark and toxic waste that hissed and fizzed at the shoreline. Jutting out over the lake's surface was a long, sturdy panel that was riveted into the ground at its base.

'You're making me walk *the plank*?' said the Doctor. 'You know, not even *pirates* made people walk the plank. Well... Earth pirates didn't, anyway. Common misconception.'

'You walk up there,' said Sancho, gesturing towards the iron jetty with his spear.

The Doctor sighed. His hands were still bound with rope, and, despite several surreptitious attempts to free himself using every trick in the book, he'd had no success. However devolved these humans were, they certainly knew how to tie a good knot, he had to give them that. Of course, he could always try and make a run for it. None of them had firearms. He'd just have to hope their aim with arrows and spears wasn't particularly good; but then he doubted that very much.

'Sancho,' he said softly. 'You don't have to do this. I can *help* you. If you'd just—'

Sancho jabbed him in the back. 'You walk up there!' he barked, more insistently than before. The other guards were growing restless, rattling their spears threateningly.

The Doctor nodded, and began walking up the ramp, out over the lake, with Sancho following him every step of the way.

When he had reached its end, the Doctor looked down into the acid of Lake Mono and took a deep breath. He had faced so many dangers before, found himself in so many situations from which there had seemed no obvious way out, and yet now he found himself stuck in a tight spot by some rope handcuffs and a handful of angry humans armed with spears. In his many lives he had fallen great heights and been shot. He'd lost a hand and grown it back. He had seen the end of the universe, and lived to tell the tale. But acid… Acid was something else. Acid would rule out a regeneration. Acid would be final.

'You will die now,' said Sancho, nudging him with the spear once more.

The Doctor closed his eyes. He thought of Amy, and he wondered where she was. Maybe there was some way out of this for *her* at least. Maybe the Sittuun would take her away, somewhere safe. Perhaps he could draw some comfort from *that*. He opened his eyes again, his toes now inching over the jetty's end. He could feel the chemical warmth rising up from the lake's surface, the noxious fumes stinging his nostrils. Looking back across the curved field of verdigris, he saw a single dark figure making its way towards the edges of the lake. It was Tuco. He had no doubt come here to witness the Doctor's execution and gloat.

'You will *die* now,' said Sancho.

The Doctor nodded. Looking down, he saw his reflection warped and shimmering in the surface of Lake Mono, and he prepared himself for death.

Chapter
12

Captain Jamal sat at the control panel, his hands held over its many buttons and dials. His eyes were closed and he breathed slow and deep, holding each breath a few seconds at a time.

He opened his small, ink-black eyes and looked up at the bomb casing itself: the giant drum fixed in place by rigid brackets; the words GENETEC-KHALID SYSTEMS printed on its side in blood-red lettering, and below them the instructions – how to activate and deactivate the bomb.

'Captain…'

Turning in his chair, he saw Dr Heeva in the entrance to the bomb chamber, her expression fraught with anguish.

'Yes, Dr Heeva?'

'Captain… I've been outside. The drums are getting *louder*. Something's happening.'

'I know.'

'We have to act now.'

Captain Jamal nodded. 'Yes. I *know*.'

'Have you heard no word from Charlie? I mean… Baasim?'

The Captain shook his head. 'No,' he replied despondently. 'No… He's so *wilful* sometimes. He takes after his mother.'

Dr Heeva looked down, as if in shame.

'And what do I tell her?' asked the Captain. 'When we get home, I mean? How do I tell her that I just left him here, to die?'

Dr Heeva crossed the room, placing one hand on the Captain's shoulder.

'Don't ask me that,' she said. 'Please… You know how difficult it is for me, talking about her. How can I answer that question?'

'No, Heeva… Please. This has nothing to do with… with *us*. I thought we'd agreed… What's happened here, in *this* place… When we've left, that's it. It's over. You know that.'

Heeva nodded, tearfully. 'Yes. I know.'

Captain Jamal closed his eyes and sighed. 'And the drums are getting louder?' he asked.

Dr Heeva nodded.

'And how long until the comet's impact?' Captain Jamal asked her.

'A hundred minutes, Captain. We have just one hundred minutes.'

They hid behind a mound of sagging metal and torn plastic in one of the city's side streets, if it could be called that. Though almost everything on the Gyre had been manufactured at some point, time had weathered it down to a point where it appeared almost organic, as if the bizarre formations rising up around them had formed naturally over millions, rather than thousands of years.

On the other side of the mound the humans were milling in all directions. There were people pushing wheelbarrows and people lugging barrels on their backs. Two men walked by with what looked like barbecued Sollogs on a long, metal skewer. From somewhere in the distance, Charlie and Amy could hear the sound of drums and tribal chanting.

'OK...' whispered Charlie. 'I can't believe that *actually* worked.'

'Well, drama *was* one of my best subjects in school,' said Amy. 'Natural performer, my teacher called me.'

Charlie nodded, smiling nervously. 'Yeah,' he said. 'That *was* pretty good, I must admit. You had *me* scared for a moment. And that guy in the watchtower fell for it hook, line and sinker. You make a convincing human.'

'Er... *Excuse* me? I *am* human.'

'Yeah, but… You know what I mean.'

They heard the sound of marching. Peering out from the side of the mound, Amy saw a platoon of humans armed with spears trudging past. They were heading towards the main gate.

'OK…' she said. 'What now?'

Charlie glanced down and shook his head. 'I don't know,' he said. 'I've never been here before. And this place is *massive*. The Doctor could be *anywhere*.'

Dr Heeva stood on the bridge of the *Beagle XXI*, and looked out through its windows at the desert of glass, and in the distance, the mountains. The fires there were growing brighter with every passing minute, and now she could hear the drums, even from inside the ship.

What were the humans doing?

She had been waiting for Captain Jamal for what felt like an eternity, having left him alone in the bomb chamber. She knew, or thought she knew, how difficult this must be for him. His only son was out there, somewhere – on his way to the human city, perhaps – and there was little chance of his return.

It was almost impossible for her to separate her feelings from the urgency of the situation, the two were so entangled. She and the Captain had comforted one another in the months following the crash. The rest of the crew were so much younger than them, and treated both the Captain and Heeva differently, with an almost parental reverence and distance, which left them somewhat isolated. It was only natural that, as the two most senior crew members, they would enjoy each other's company.

Now that there was a chance for them to leave and survive this nightmare, she didn't know what to think. What would life back on their home planet be like? Would she ever see Jamal again? Would they be able to talk about anything that had happened on the Gyre? When he was back with his wife, would he find some way to blame Heeva for his son's death, some way to take his feelings of guilt and transplant them onto somebody else? A part of her, just a small part, wished that she had gone out there instead of Charlie. If she had taken the helipod, Charlie would have had no other option but to leave with his father. At least then nobody could have blamed her for anything.

The entrance to the deck slid open with a hiss, and Captain Jamal stepped into the room. He braced himself against the door frame, his head hung in shame.

'I can't do it,' he said. 'He's my *son*. If we can just wait… Thirty minutes…'

'But *Captain*…'

'Please, Heeva. I'll prepare Slipstream's ship. Just let me wait another thirty minutes.'

Dr Heeva nodded and looked out from the bridge across the desert of glass. There, in the valleys to the east, she saw the orange light of distant fires flickering against the metal hills. Just thirty minutes, the Captain had said.

But did they really have that long?

Chapter
13

'Oh... We're back here, then?' said the Doctor.

Sancho, his guard, sneered at him with a sideways glance.

They were in the throne room at the top of the decaying and ramshackle tower, the torches and fluorescent tubes flickering around them. Django and Tuco were already on the platform, beneath the faded, grinning face of Gobo the Clown.

'Your life has been spared,' rasped Tuco. 'You are very lucky.'

'Yes, funny that,' said the Doctor, with sarcasm. 'You see, Sancho here was about a split second away from pushing me into a pit of acid (don't worry, Sancho... No hard feelings) and you still haven't told me *why* I was spared.'

He heard the sound of shuffling feet, a slow and steady march, and more humans entered the throne room, bringing with them a man in a silver spacesuit. The latter walked straight up to the Doctor, holding out his hand.

'The Doctor, I presume!' he said with a gleaming smile. 'Spiffing to see you again!'

The Doctor frowned. 'I'm sorry…' he said. 'Have we met?'

'Oh dear,' said the man in the spacesuit. 'Please don't say you can't remember me. That would be *frightfully* awkward, wouldn't it?'

The Doctor's eyes grew wide and his jaw dropped. 'Oh no,' he groaned. 'Dirk Slipstream.'

'At your service!' said Slipstream, still grinning. The Doctor still hadn't shaken his hand, so he dropped it to his side.

From the platform, Tuco had been watching this scene with reptilian fascination and a quizzical scowl, but now he stepped down and approached them.

'You… *know* each other?'

The Doctor nodded and sighed. 'Yes,' he said. 'We've met before.' He turned to Slipstream. 'Last time I saw you, you were behind bars… *rightfully* behind bars… on Volag-Noc.'

'I know!' said Slipstream, still smiling graciously. 'And you were the chap who put me there. Remember that?'

'Yes. Yes, I do. The Belaform Diamond Heist.' The Doctor turned to Tuco. 'This man crashed a passenger ship into a diamond depository on Belaform 9. Killed six hundred passengers and a hundred people at the depository, just to steal some jewels.'

'My finest work,' said Slipstream, beaming proudly. 'The perfect crime. Or at least it would have been, if you hadn't interfered. Still, Doctor. Let bygones be bygones is my motto. After all, we've both changed. *You've* changed considerably. Had some work done?'

The Doctor glowered at Slipstream. It was then that he noticed Manco standing behind him, surrounded by the small army of human guards.

'Manco!' he said, suddenly a little more relieved. 'What are you doing here?'

'He is your guide,' hissed Tuco, before Manco had a chance to speak.

'Guide?' asked the Doctor. 'What do you mean, "guide"?'

He turned to Slipstream, who winked back at him. 'Going on a field trip, old chap. And you're tagging along for the ride. You see, your services are of use to me. That's why I had to reel you in with the old trans-temporal distress signal. Knew you'd never come if I just asked politely.'

'It was *you*...' said the Doctor, his brow furrowing with resentment.

'Oh yes. I knew if there was one man who'd pick that signal up sooner or later it was the Doctor. I stayed in geostationary orbit around the Gyre waiting to pick up your signal. And look... Here you are! And not a minute too soon.'

From his throne, Django now rose to his feet. His tall, angular frame towering over the other humans as he stepped down from the platform, his grubby white robes billowing behind him. He brushed his way past his guards and approached Slipstream.

'And now,' he purred huskily, 'you tell us where the Sittuun are hiding.'

They had made it perhaps fifty metres further into the city before they had to hide again. Something was happening, that was for sure. The streets were a hive of activity now, with more and more armed soldiers gathering near the gates. What were they doing?

Looking up, Amy saw that she and Charlie were at the base of the wrecked spacecraft. Its colossal bulk towered above them, piercing the wisps of grey-green cloud that drifted over the Gyre.

Beyond the stark, black outline of the wreck, too bright to look at for more than a second, the Schuler-Khan comet grew bigger still. Just looking at it made Amy shudder. But there was something else in the sky. Something that seemed to break away from Schuler-Khan's dazzling orb, dropping down towards the Gyre with its own flickering tail of fire trailing out behind it.

'What's *that*?' asked Amy.

'What's what?'

Amy nodded towards the sky. '*That*,' she said.

'Oh...' gasped Charlie. 'That's not good.'

Suddenly, there was a loud bang, like the sound of a firework or a cannon being fired. The streak of light punched its way through a cloud, and was now rumbling through the sky with a thunderous drum roll which grew louder and louder, until it was almost deafening. Amy cupped her ears with her hands and closed her eyes as tightly as she could.

Seconds later the ground convulsed, as if somebody, some unimaginable giant, had taken hold of the Gyre and shaken it with both hands. Fragments of junk rained down from the structures of the human city, and they heard a cacophony of screams echoing through its streets.

'What was it?' cried Amy.

'It was a fragment of the comet,' said Charlie. 'It's started.'

'That was just a *fragment*?' said Amy, a little louder than she'd intended.

Charlie nodded.

From the watchtowers they now heard the blasting of horns, each overlapping the other, forming a discordant drone that howled out over the city's rooftops, but in the streets around them something else was happening. Peering out from behind a rusting metal crate, Amy saw a large door in a nearby building opening up, and a group of humans spilled out. Leading them was Slipstream.

'He's here!' she whispered. 'Slipstream. I can see him.'

Then she saw another face she recognised.

'And they've got the Doctor!'

The procession made its way along the street, heading towards the towering wreck. When they reached it, one of the humans began tapping away at a control panel.

'We have to do something, Charlie! We have to save him!'

Charlie held Amy's shoulder and pulled her back.

'What can we do?' he said. 'There's dozens of them. If we jump out now they'll *kill* us.'

Amy struggled free of his grasp, but didn't dare move more than a few inches, so that she could watch the scene once more. Next to the control panel, a large metal hatch opened up, the door coming away on mechanical hinges that groaned and creaked as if they hadn't been used in centuries. Slipstream, the Doctor, and three more humans entered, and then the rest of the humans moved on, rushing down the street towards the city gates.

'This is our chance,' said Amy. 'We've got to do *something*...'

'So... Manco, old chap. Which way?'

The five of them were deep inside the wreck, making their way along a corridor tilted at such an angle that they had to walk along its corner. Sancho had, until now, led the group, carrying a burning torch, and they had come to a junction of three more corridors.

'It would help if I knew what you were looking for,' said Manco.

Tuco brushed past and approached Slipstream.

'Yes, Mr Slipstream. Tuco would *also* like to know what you are looking for...'

Slipstream eyed Tuco with a look of disdain, his lip curling up into a sneer, and he sighed through gritted teeth.

'Is there *really* any need for you to be here?' he hissed.

'Oh yes,' said Tuco. 'Yes. Tuco must be here. You have the heretics with you. Django wants Tuco here. To *watch* them.'

'And must you *always* refer to yourself in the third person? It's a tad egomaniacal, old bean.'

'Tuco does not understand "third person".'

'No. I doubt Tuco would. So... Manco... As I was *saying*. Which way?'

Manco bit his lip. He looked to the Doctor with a helpless expression, nervously lowering his eyes, before turning to Slipstream once more. 'And as *I* was saying, it would help if I knew what you were looking for.'

Slipstream laughed casually, rolling his eyes. 'The hold,' he said. 'We're looking for the hold. Where they kept the cargo. Do you understand that word? Cargo?'

Manco nodded. 'It's this way,' he said, pointing straight ahead.

They moved on. At no point did the Doctor take his eyes off Slipstream. How could he not have recognised him the moment he saw him? But then, to the Doctor, so many years and regenerations had passed since they last met. To Slipstream, it may only have been a few short years, or even months.

On their last meeting, the Doctor had been too late to stop him from committing his crime. The ship had crashed and hundreds of people had died. The only thing the Doctor could do was stop him before he made his escape with literally millions of precious stones, but stop him he had. He had stood in the courthouse as Slipstream was sentenced to one hundred years imprisonment for every one of his victims; seventy thousand years in all, a sentence he could never hope to survive. Unless, of course, he escaped.

And now Slipstream had given the humans

the location of the Sittuun hideout. As Tuco and Sancho had taken them out of the throne room, Django was already planning his attack.

Chapter
14

The dazzling light from Schuler-Khan reflected off the crystal surface of the great salt plains, making it look almost like an ocean on a summer's day. The human city was far behind them now, as they made their way west.

From a distance, at the edges of the swamp, they would have appeared as a shimmering mirage; the dark line of humans, some marching and some riding great clunking, wheezing contraptions, powered by steam or by levers, like handcars from the distant, Earth-bound past. It would have been silent at first, this shimmering apparition on the horizon, framed between the twinkling white desert and the dark black silhouette of the tower. Then, slowly, the sound of the humans' progress would grow louder: the crunching of a hundred pairs of feet on salt crystals; the rusty whine of turning wheels and the mechanical thump and hiss of the engines.

Sat on top of the largest vehicle was Django, his throne transplanted from its chamber onto a machine that propelled itself along on eight mechanical legs. His long, scraggly hair and bedraggled robes rippled in the breeze behind him, giving him the appearance of a human flagpole or a mascot.

His face was caked in thick make-up. His skin was a deathly shade of white, his mouth framed with a garish crimson smile and his eyes with bright blue hoops. Dark black lines like sickles arched up on his forehead.

His gaze was fixed firmly on the horizon, beyond the swaying plastic tubes of the swamp. Django smiled maniacally and gnashed his teeth. He looked skywards, to the burning light of the star that grew ever bigger above him, staring into its light until it hurt his eyes, and tears were streaming down his cheeks. The tears drew jagged streaks of blue and red across his face as they fell.

If there was only some way he could send a warning. Something that might alert the Sittuun…

The Doctor hadn't spoken for some time. The five of them – Tuco, Sancho, Manco, Slipstream and the

Doctor – had passed through numerous passages, climbing flights of stairs and metal ladders. In one room they had found nothing but glass sleep pods, each one containing a skeleton. The higher they climbed, the more they heard the wind howling through the rusting hulk. Sometimes the howling would stop, and there would be an eerie silence but for their footsteps. Then, every once in a while, they would hear the sound of something crashing in the distance, and the ground beneath them would shake.

The Doctor paid little attention to any of these sights and sounds. His mind was working overtime. Amy was out there, somewhere. Amy Pond from Leadworth. What was a girl from Leadworth doing in a place like this? If she was with the Sittuun, then she was in danger. He had to warn them. He had to get out of the human city and back to the TARDIS. He had to at least *try* and convince the humans to save themselves, or allow him to save them. So many things to consider, and so little time.

'Say, Slipstream…' he said, stomping up to the front of the group. 'This *thing*… that you need my assistance with?'

'Yes?' Slipstream looked at him with one eyebrow arched.

'What is it? What are we *looking* for, exactly?'

Slipstream sighed. 'I don't think you'd believe me if I told you, old chap.'

'Try me.'

'Very well. We are looking for the Mymon Key.'

The Doctor gasped. 'But… but that's *impossible*.'

Slipstream started laughing, his laughter echoing along the corridor and deep into the bowels of the ship. 'Oh, that's *priceless*, Doctor. Really, it is. You're the last of your kind, and you still manage to toe the party line, even when there's no party left.'

Manco was looking at them both and frowning. 'What is the Mymon Key?' he asked.

The Doctor turned to him. 'The Mymon Key was an energy source. A limitless energy source. Forged on Mercutio 14 by the Hexion Geldmongers. Whoever owned the Mymon Key would have the power to do *anything*. It drew its power from gravitational force. It could drive a ship safely through a black hole. It could be used to tear the fabric of the universe apart. Wars were fought over it. *Endless* wars. Nobody had the right to that kind of power.'

Slipstream nodded, grinning. 'That's the one!' he said, cheerily.

'But the Mymon Key was destroyed…'

Slipstream shook his head. 'No, Doctor. Not *destroyed*. It was taken back. When they realised the damage their masterpiece had caused, the Hexion Geldmongers took it back to Mercutio 14 and locked it inside a casket, an intricate puzzle box.'

'But…' The Doctor was breathing heavily now,

shaking his head and running his hands through his hair. 'The wars didn't end there. Mercutio 14 was attacked. It was destroyed. The Mymon Key was destroyed with it.'

Slipstream patted the Doctor's shoulder playfully, still smiling. ''Fraid not, Doctor. You see, that's the thing with wars. All that chaos and confusion. Seems the casket was seized before its makers were wiped out. Only problem was, the Geldmongers were a crafty lot. Only somebody fluent in Hexion could unlock the casket, rendering its contents quite worthless. It found its way to a museum of antiquities back in the thirty-first century. From what I can gather, there were budget cuts, you know how things are. The casket was sold to a private buyer in Andromeda. It was in transit when the ship carrying it simply vanished. Pfff! Like *that*.'

'This ship...' the Doctor whispered.

Slipstream nodded. 'Well done, Doctor. Not just a pretty face, are you?'

'And how do *you* know all this?'

'Well, Doctor, for all of its many faults – the knuckle-headed guards, the freezing cold, the *dreadful* food – Volag-Noc does have a rather splendid library. Awful lot of potboilers and bad thrillers, of course, but the history section was *superb*. I was looking at a seventy-thousand-year stretch, Doctor. Plenty of time to read.'

The Doctor shook his head, his eyes screwed shut. 'And you sold out the Sittuun for *this*?'

Slipsteam leaned in close to the Doctor and spoke in a conspiratorial whisper.

'I wouldn't worry too much about *them*, Doctor. That canyon? To the west? Only bridge across it is gone, I'm afraid. Kaput. Those savages won't get far.'

Eventually they came to the end of another corridor, and passing through a large hatch they found themselves in a cavernous room, flanked on both sides with enormous glass screens, each one blank, lifeless and grey. The hatch led out onto a narrow walkway, below which the room fell away, perhaps thirty metres beneath them. They were in the nerve centre of the ship, the control room. Thousands of years earlier, it would have been filled with crew members, hundreds of them. Now it was home to nothing more than tangled vines and swirling clouds of dust.

'This is the room,' said Manco. 'The one I told you about. The screens… they don't work.'

'Oh, we'll see about that,' said the Doctor.

He marched along the walkway, past Tuco and Sancho, until he reached a bank of consoles, which he studied for a moment.

'Doctor…' said Slipstream. 'We've no time for fun and games.'

'See this?' said the Doctor, pointing at his face.

'This is me concentrating. Which means it's your turn to shut up.'

Slipstream lifted his gun. 'See this, Doctor? This is a gun. Which means you'll do as I say.'

The Doctor smiled. 'Nice try, Slipstream,' he said. 'But you *need* me, remember? Now this won't take a moment...'

Before Slipstream could say another word, the Doctor had his sonic screwdriver aimed straight at the console. It buzzed into life, and all at once the console was lit up with flashing lights.

'What is he *doing*?' hissed Tuco. 'The tower is *sacred*. The tower is the home of Gobo!'

Sancho marched towards the Doctor, raising his spear, but then, one by one, the giant screens that lined the walls of the control room flickered on, each one showing nothing but fizzing white static. Sancho froze.

At the console the Doctor tapped at keys and flicked switches, and the screens turned from a jittering blizzard to a single, vibrant shade of blue. The Doctor hit a final switch, and the blue became the image of a man, his face repeated dozens of times the length of the room. The man wore the khaki uniform of a pilot, his surname, Velasquez, stencilled onto his chest.

'I am Captain Zachary Velasquez, of the Gobocorp Freight Company,' he said, his voice booming and echoing in the cathedral-like space.

'What is this?' bellowed Tuco, seething and clutching at the handrail with his bony fingers.

Velasquez continued: 'The GFC *Herald of Nanking* has crash-landed on this world, at the outer edge of Battani 045. Of our 3,000-strong crew, only 500 are left. If you are watching this, there is every chance that we are all dead. Earth is twenty-five light years away, and our location remote. May God have mercy on our souls.'

The Doctor hit a button. The image on the screens fizzed and crackled, and then they turned once more to that brilliant shade of blue. Breathing heavily through his nostrils, Tuco turned to the Doctor.

'What is this *outrage*?' he howled. 'What heresy is this? Doctor? Tell me!'

The Doctor turned to Tuco, pocketing his sonic screwdriver. 'I'm so sorry. It's who you are. You're the survivors.'

Tuco shook his head and tore at his robes with clawed fingernails, his voice reduced to an anguished wail.

By his side, Sancho looked out across the chamber full of glowing blue screens with an expression of horror.

'E-earth?' he stuttered. 'This isn't... this isn't Earth?'

The Doctor shook his head.

'But... but... he said "ship". The man... the man

said *ship*. He said they crashed here. And Gobocorp. What is Gobocorp?'

The Doctor turned back to the console and pressed another button. Once again the screens came to life with the image of Captain Velasquez. The Doctor twisted a dial, speeding through the last few seconds of the video, and now they saw the image of an animated clown, Gobo, carrying a parcel. The clown placed the parcel on the ground, opened it, and a bright red balloon came floating out. As the balloon rose up into the air, the Gobo popped it with a needle, and the word 'GOBOCORP' appeared in its place.

'Gobocorp!' said a big and cheerful voice which echoed across the room. 'For *all* your delivery needs, go Gobocorp!'

Sancho turned away, closing his eyes as if to block out what he had seen.

'No…' he whimpered. 'No…'

Then he turned to Tuco.

'You *lied* to us,' he raged. 'You… Django… Lies. It was all lies. Must tell the others. Must tell *everyone*.'

Tuco glowered at Sancho, shaking his head, the spittle in the corners of his mouth whipped into a foam.

'No!' he screeched, charging towards the guard. 'No!'

With terrifying violence, Tuco struck Sancho

across the head with his cane, dazing him and, in one ferocious move, he pushed him over the side of the walkway, sending him tumbling down into the depths of the control room, where he landed with a heavy thud.

It happened so quickly the Doctor had no chance to intervene. 'No!' he shouted. 'Tuco! What have you *done*?'

'You see?' said Tuco. 'This is how the heresy spreads. You, Doctor! You are to blame!'

He lifted his cane once more, preparing to launch himself at the Doctor, but found himself staring down the barrel of Slipstream's gun.

'Don't think so, Tuco, old chap. We've wasted enough time. Let's move on.'

Braced against the console, the Doctor let out a long shuddering breath. Slipstream was ushering Tuco and Manco along, still aiming the gun. He turned now to the Doctor.

'You too, Doctor,' he said.

Unseen by Slipstream or the others, the Doctor hit one last switch before they left.

Chapter
15

Captain Jamal sat at the controls of the *Golden Bough*. He'd never flown a ship like this before. The thing was practically an antique, and it was neither a military nor a commercial craft, that was for sure. This was the kind of ship that men like Dirk Slipstream flew for no other reason than to show off. *Hot rods*, they called them. An old Earth term, apparently. Sure, it was probably fast and it would turn enough heads, but the thing was of little practical use.

The controls were so archaic he was vaguely surprised to find an autopilot. Still, he was pretty sure he had it all figured out. Now if he could only bring himself to call Dr Heeva to the ship and take off, make that final move. Leave the Gyre.

But it wasn't just a case of leaving the Gyre. If that was all it came down to, he'd have activated the bomb and left right away. No, something else was keeping him here, stopping him from leaving. His anger had subsided now, and in its place he felt something strange and unsettling. An emotion that was different to anything he had felt before. If he hadn't known better, he would have thought it was a human emotion. *Fear*.

'Captain Jamal!'

The voice of Dr Heeva spoke to him from the cockpit's intercom.

'Yes, Dr Heeva. What is it?'

He looked up from the windscreen of the *Golden Bough* towards the deck of the *Beagle XXI*. Dr Heeva was standing in its windows, holding the microphone to her mouth.

'There's a signal, Captain. It's coming from the human city.'

'What kind of a signal?'

'It looks like Morse code, sir.'

'Morse code? Who uses Morse code these days?'

'I don't know. I can barely make it out. There's a flashing light... Looks like it's coming from the tower; from the old wreck. But I can't read Morse code.'

'OK, Heeva. Read it out to me. Tell me what it says.'

One by one Dr Heeva read out the dots and dashes of the signal, and one by one Captain Jamal translated them into letters.

'H... u... m... a... n... s... a... t... t... a... c... k... i...'

That was when he was stopped. At the other end of the line, Dr Heeva was silent. He looked up at her once more.

'It's the humans...' gasped Captain Jamal. 'The humans are coming.'

Dr Heeva nodded, closing her eyes. 'Then *I'll* do it,' she said.

'Do what?'

'I'll activate the bomb.'

They were surrounded by Sollogs on all sides. The monstrous slimy creatures slithered through the stagnant green waters of the swamp and scuttled from pipe to pipe, drawing around them in an ever-tightening circle. Some of their vehicles had proven useless crossing the swamp, and had been left on the salt flat. Others, such as the contraption carrying Django on his throne, were more robust.

Django looked around, at the swarming Sollogs, and he bared his teeth and snarled at them. Around him, his men fought with the creatures, lunging at them and skewering them with spears, or shooting them with arrows, but they were outnumbered.

As all hope seemed lost, there came from the

sky a series of loud crashing sounds, each one more deafening than the last.

Django looked up from his throne and saw, high above, what looked like falling stars, tearing through the dark blue sky – so bright it looked as if the night itself had been ripped into shreds. The falling stars passed over the swamp, heading east, and then there was a sound like thunder, and the ground beneath them shook. The plastic tubes that shot up from the surface of the swamp clanked and rattled, and the waters sloshed around their legs.

The Sollogs were startled, their attack on the humans forgotten in an instant. They scurried in all directions, breaking from their packs.

Django began to laugh.

'A miracle!' he roared, then pointed east to the far side of the swamp. 'We move on!'

They marched on through the swamp, hacking away at the plastic tubes with their swords and spears, until at last they reached the edge of the canyon. Half of the metal pipe that had been a makeshift bridge was still hanging from their side of the gorge, but over on the other side they saw the point where the fallen stars had crashed.

The high cliffs to either side of the distant gully were beginning to collapse: mountains of refuse hundreds of metres tall now crumbling, sending countless tons of metal plummeting down into the canyon.

Django stood up from his throne, holding his hands towards the sky. His army could only look on, as the canyon before them began to disappear, its dark void filled with the falling wreckage. Great clouds of dust and smoke billowed up from the chaos and the noise below them, and Django was laughing.

When it had stopped, and the dust had settled, they saw before them not an impassable gulf, but a shallow trench.

'Witness!' shouted Django. 'Witness the might of Gobo! We move on!'

At his order, the humans marched on, down into the shallow ravine and ever closer to the Sittuun's hiding place.

Several storeys below the bridge of the *Beagle XXI*, the Nanobomb sat in its chamber. The room was silent and still, and would have been completely dark had it not been illuminated by the light from the bomb's counter. The digits counted down, second by second.

00:59:23...
00:59:22...
00:59:21...

Chapter
16

The cargo hold of the GFS *Herald of Nanking* was vast. No, the Doctor decided. Vast was too small a word. Four letters, one syllable. Vast was far too small. Humungous was getting there, but still didn't do it justice. As they entered the cavernous space, with Tuco now carrying the flaming torch, their voices echoed out into the gloom, bouncing through deep gullies of crates and containers.

'Crikey,' said the Doctor. 'It'll be like finding a needle in a haystack. Or rather, it'll be like finding one specific needle in a pile of near-identical needles.'

With the ship having crashed at such an angle – its front half buried in the Gyre and the whole ship turned slightly on its side – the cargo hold was like the inside of a cube balanced perfectly on one corner. Most of its contents had been sent tumbling down to one end of the room, where the containers lay in a disorganised mound.

'Not necessarily, Doctor,' said Slipstream, producing a small hardbound book from his pocket. He flipped it open, licked his thumb, and began flicking through the pages.

'This book lists all of the passengers, crew and contents for the *Herald of Nanking* on the day she went missing. Only thing it doesn't have is schematics. Seems the *Herald of Nanking* was quite the mystery, back in the day. A small army of obsessive enthusiasts would pore over her every last detail and concoct all manner of outlandish theories to explain her disappearance. And this book lists not only the contents of the ship, but also their location.'

Slipstream craned his head back, looking up into the far corner of the room.

'I say... Tuco, old chap, could you lift the torch a little higher? You're hogging all the light.'

With a derisive grunt, Tuco lifted the torch. The feeble light spread itself a little further into the room, pushing back the shadows.

'Up there,' said Slipstream. 'Row F. Level 3. Let's get climbing.'

Like mountaineers in the foothills of a mountain range, the four of them set about climbing up over the rugged landscape of shattered crates and debris, past stacks and shelves that had buckled and sagged after millennia of neglect. From somewhere, out beyond the ship's hull, they heard another thunderous boom. The room shook violently, flakes of orange rust raining down from the ceiling. The Doctor felt both of his hearts beating faster than before.

'So, Slipstream...' he said.

'Yes, Doctor?'

'When we're done here, when you've got what you want, we're leaving, yes?'

Slipstream shrugged. 'Wish it was up to me, old chap,' he said. 'I only arranged for you to be spared *today*. Didn't quite have the clout to get you off all charges, I'm afraid. What say you, Tuco? When we're finished, can the Doctor leave?'

'No,' Tuco snapped. 'He is a heretic and a prisoner of Django. He will be thrown into Lake Mono.'

'Ah, see?' said Slipstream. 'Sorry, Doctor. Them's the breaks, as they say. Damned nuisance. Can't say I envy you.'

The Doctor turned to Tuco. 'Tuco... Listen to me. In another hour or two, there won't *be* a Lake Mono. You hear those noises outside?'

Tuco shrugged; a gesture almost of denial.

'But you *can* hear them. Can't you?'

'Maybe.'

'That noise is the sound of little bits of comet slamming into this place, tearing it apart. I'm talking *little* bits of comet. About this big?' He held his finger and thumb no more than three inches apart. 'The comet... I mean the *actual* comet... Is hundreds of *metres* across. Bigger than this room. When it hits us, this world will be destroyed. Everyone will die. Do you understand that?'

Tuco looked at him coldly, narrowing his eyes. 'Then it is the way of Gobo,' he growled with a sinister smile.

As they climbed further up towards the high corner of the cargo hold, Manco walked beside the Doctor.

'It's no use,' he said. 'They won't listen. They *never* listen.'

They were halfway up the mountain of upturned crates when they heard something fluttering around their heads. It sounded to the Doctor like moths on a summer's night, hovering towards the nearest source of light. They halted abruptly, none of them daring to move. Tuco's face was frozen with alarm, the hand in which he carried the torch shaking.

Something small passed between the Doctor and the flickering light; something tiny and dark and silhouetted against the flame.

Tuco jumped, losing his footing and falling onto his back. The torch landed beside him, but the flame carried on burning.

Now the Doctor could see more of the flying creatures, none of them any bigger than his thumb. He crouched down beside where Tuco had fallen, squinting at them in the dim light. Lifting it from the ground the Doctor moved the flame through the stygian gloom, and saw dozens, perhaps hundreds, of tiny airborne forms.

One of them came right up to his face, hovering before him with its wings flapping into a blur. The creature was limbless, but for its wings; its scaly body was a golden shade of orange, its eyes like tiny silver pennies. Its mouth tapered away into what looked like a beak.

'Hello!' said the Doctor, holding up his hand and offering it a gentle wave.

'What the *devil* is that?' Slipstream gasped, looking at the creature with an expression of disgust.

'I *think* it's a fish,' said the Doctor. 'A flying fish. Literally.'

From his side he heard the sound of Slipstream's blaster powering up – a thin whining sound that rose in pitch. Slipstream lifted the gun, and aimed it straight for the tiny flying fish.

'Blasted pests!' he barked. 'Planet's infested with 'em. If it's not the savages it's eight-legged slugs, and if it's not them it's a flying piranha!'

Before Slipstream could fire, the Doctor reached

out, grabbed the gun by its barrel, and gently steered his aim away from the fish.

'Does it *look* like a piranha to you?' he asked. 'Look around you. Do you spot much in the way of meat? And look at Tuco. He's never seen one of these things before. They must only live in here, inside the ship.'

Tuco was on his feet again, brushing the dust and flakes of brown rust from his clothes. All at once the flying fish swarmed around him, nibbling at the air like goldfish taking their food from the surface of a fish tank.

'What are they doing?' Tuco growled, squirming with displeasure.

'The rust,' said the Doctor. 'They're eating the rust.'

'I still say we should kill 'em,' Slipstream snapped. 'Just in case.'

'Yes, well you *would*. But not everything here is as mean-spirited as you.'

Slipstream scowled at him and, for the first time since they had become reacquainted, the Doctor could sense the simmering resentment beneath Slipstream's cool, suave exterior. However cordial he might be playing this, Slipstream clearly wasn't here to let 'bygones be bygones', as he had put it. When all this was over, when they had found the Mymon Key, Slipstream would no doubt look for his revenge.

They heard another crash from outside the ship. This one sounded closer than any they had heard before.

'Come on,' said the Doctor, holding up the torch and leading the way. 'Let's find your key.'

As the light around them grew dimmer, Slipstream, Manco and Tuco followed him. Up and up they climbed, the incline of spilt containers getting steeper, until at last they reached the upper corner of the room.

'Here it is,' announced Slipstream. 'Row F. Level 3.'

He seized the torch from the Doctor's hand, and began to navigate his way around the buckled shelves and fallen crates.

'It must be here somewhere...'

The others could only stand there and watch him. Somewhere beyond the cargo hold and the ship there was another thunderous boom. The Doctor looked at Manco and then at Tuco, who was still watching him with simmering malevolence. With Slipstream distracted by his search for the casket, maybe this was his opportunity. Maybe he and Manco could make a run for it. With Sancho gone, they could get past Tuco easily enough. They could leave the cargo hold and the ship, and escape from the human city. Maybe they could find their way to the Sittuun, and Amy, before it was all too late.

But something was keeping him there. A feeling he didn't want to acknowledge. It was curiosity. The Doctor *wanted* to see the casket and its contents. He *needed* to see it. Mercutio 14 was now no more than a burnt and barren rock, devoid of life. The Hexion Geldmongers had been extinct for millennia. The Mymon Key, their greatest and most terrible creation, was the stuff of legends. He had to see it. That was what was keeping him there.

'I've found it,' Slipstream gasped, his voice trembling with emotion. 'I've *found* it.'

The Doctor ran to his side and looked over his shoulder. Then he saw it: the gleaming cobalt box, its lustre only slightly tarnished by the thin film of dust on its surface.

Slipstream swept over it with his hand, and now the Doctor saw the markings on its surface – an ancient language that hadn't been written down or spoken in hundreds of thousands of years.

'Give it to me,' said the Doctor.

Slipstream lifted the casket, which was no bigger than a shoebox, free of the cluttered mound of fallen crates, and looked back at the Doctor, smiling awkwardly.

'What did you say?'

'I said give it to me.'

Slipstream frowned quizzically, as if taken aback by the Doctor's tone, and then the Doctor reached forward and seized the box from his grasp.

The Doctor ran his hands around the casket, his fingers tracing their way through the intricate markings. He held the casket up to his ear as if listening out for something the others simply couldn't hear. He shook the box, and listened to it once more.

'It's broken,' he said.

'Well, I'm not surprised, old bean,' snapped Slipstream. 'What with you shaking it about like that.'

'No… It's always been broken. The whole time it's been here.'

'What do you mean, *broken*? The key?'

'No… Not the key. The casket. The anti-gravitational field isn't working. The key… the key has been working the whole time.'

Slipstream stood at his side and pointed at the markings. 'And this?' he said. 'Can you read this?'

The Doctor nodded reluctantly. 'You know I can.'

'And what does it say?'

'They're instructions,' the Doctor replied. 'But you knew that already.'

'Perhaps I did. Then I'd suggest you follow them, Doctor. *Follow* the instructions and open the casket.'

The Doctor shook his head. 'I can't,' he whispered. 'I can't let you have the Mymon Key. It's too powerful.'

Slipstream lifted his blaster and placed its barrel squarely against the Doctor's head.

'Open the damned casket,' he snarled. 'I won't ask you a second time.'

He could see them now, blazing towards them in a shimmering cloud of dust; the dark mass of humans tearing their way across the desert of glass.

The engines of the *Golden Bough* roared into life with a terrific whoosh and the whole ship shuddered.

'Dr Heeva,' said Captain Jamal, speaking into the intercom. 'What is your location?'

'I'm on Deck 3.'

'Then *hurry*. They're almost here. We *have* to get out of here!'

He looked back across the glistening desert, and saw the black haze separating out, the individual forms of the humans and their ancient, makeshift vehicles becoming visible. Somewhere in amongst the mob he saw a single figure riding on an arachnoid, eight-legged vehicle – a figure dressed in flowing white robes – and he knew instantly it must be their leader.

'Please, Dr Heeva... *Hurry!*'

Heeva came running from the loading bay door, but stopped at its control panel and began hitting the keys.

'What are you doing?' the Captain hissed into

the intercom.

'I'm closing the doors,' said Dr Heeva. 'If we leave them open, the humans will get to the bomb. They might be able to deactivate it. We have to close the doors.'

'There isn't time.'

'Then go.'

'I can't. I won't leave without you.'

Dr Heeva turned from the control panel and looked up at him. There were tears streaming from her small black eyes and rolling down her pallid, grey cheeks.

'Please,' she said. 'Just go.'

Captain Jamal closed his eyes. From beyond the hull of the *Golden Bough*, he could hear the sound of Schuler-Khan's fragments slamming into the Gyre. And he could hear the humans, their machines clanking and hissing, and their heavy feet stomping as they ran. They bellowed and they hollered, their animal cries echoing out into the perpetual night.

Heeva continued hitting keys on the control panel, turning her head every so often to watch the humans' progress. The hatch began to rise up, like a metal jaw, but then the control panel exploded in a shower of sparks, and Heeva jumped back, startled, to see the shaft of an arrow jutting from its smouldering remains.

Captain Jamal rose from his seat, pounding his fists against the window.

'Get out of there!' he roared. 'Get out of there *now*!'

Heeva turned, looking up at him, and she smiled. A sad smile of resignation. The second arrow hit her in the chest, sending her reeling back against the hull of the *Beagle XXI*, and she slumped forward, falling to her knees. Seconds later, the humans were upon her.

Captain Jamal could do nothing but fall back into his seat and hit the thrusters once more. With a monstrous roar, the *Golden Bough* rose up from the surface of the Gyre, spinning round on its axis. Below it the seething black mass of humans swarmed towards the *Beagle XXI* and, for just a few seconds, the Captain saw their leader staring up at him, his face caked in gaudy, clown-like make-up.

He was laughing.

The casket's exterior was a puzzle in itself; a puzzle crafted millennia ago by a race who were now extinct.

With Slipstream's gun still trained on his head, the Doctor slid the last piece of the puzzle into place, the tiny cobalt tile moving smoothly along a groove and stopping with a click. From inside the box he heard the turning of cogs, a low whirring sound, and then the casket opened. Its panels slid away and fanned out, like the wings of a butterfly emerging from its chrysalis.

There, resting in an intricately moulded block of quartz, was the Mymon Key.

'Let me see it!' snapped Slipstream.

Holstering his gun, he snatched the casket from the Doctor's grasp and lifted out the Key, holding it up to the light. It was unfeasibly small: a block of gold the shape of a pebble, in the centre of which was a single aperture. Tuco and Manco were beside him now, staring at the Key in awe.

'Hard to believe, isn't it?' said Slipstream. 'That something so small could hold so much power.'

'Too much power,' said the Doctor coldly.

'Oh, really, old chap? This, coming from the man who travels in time and space, interfering with historical events? Bit rich, don't you think?'

'Even its creators realised their mistake,' said the Doctor. 'Why do you think they locked it away?'

'Yes, curious that, Doctor. They locked it away. They didn't *destroy* it. They locked it in a box that could only be opened by one of their own. Or, indeed, by someone such as yourself. Somewhat ironic, don't you think? If you hadn't foiled my plans on Belaform, we'd have never met. If we'd never met, I wouldn't have known of your *vast* knowledge and your legendary command of alien languages. I'd never have thought to reel you in, and none of this would have been possible. Funny how things turn out, isn't it?'

'And what will *you* do with it?'

'Oh, what *won't* I do with it, Doctor? A limitless energy source? Where does one begin? I could *start* by holding every planet and colony in Sol 1 to ransom. Think of it as a kind of taxation. Ten per cent of net profits on *all* industries or I turn the sun into a black hole. How does that sound?'

'You're insane…'

'Dear me, Doctor. Insane? Is that the best you have to offer? I would have thought it takes absolute clarity of mind to think as I do. Now come along… We literally haven't got all day.'

Slipstream pocketed the Mymon Key and drew his gun from its holster, gesturing with it towards the lower end of the cargo hold. With careful, tentative steps the four of them made their way back down the uneven slope of upturned containers, their path barely illuminated by the torch. As their footsteps stirred up clouds of ancient dust, the flying fish swarmed around them, nibbling at the air.

'So, Slipstream…' said the Doctor, 'Did you ever stop to think about why the Gyre is flat?'

'I'm sorry, old chap… What do you mean?'

'Well… This place isn't the *only* pile of junk in the universe. But it's the only one that's flat.'

'Hadn't given it much thought, to tell you the truth. Astrophysics is more your area of expertise.'

'Well, then, maybe you've wondered why the *Herald of Nanking* crashed here in the first place.'

'Again, Doctor… Such considerations are for

academics, not me.'

'Of course. But, you see, places like this – galactic junk piles – they form in perfect locations. Points in the universe where the gravitational forces of all neighbouring stars and planets converge.'

'Yes, Doctor.' Slipstream sighed. 'All very interesting, I'm sure…'

'And the Mymon Key draws its energy from gravitational force.'

'Yes? And?'

'Which would make this the perfect home for the Mymon Key.'

Slipstream clucked his tongue against the roof of his mouth.

'Ever the sentimentalist,' he muttered. 'So you're saying this place is the Mymon Key's *home*? That this inanimate lump of metal is *happy* here?'

The Doctor shrugged. 'Yes,' he said. 'I suppose I am.'

'Oh, *please*. Really? Dear oh dear… Of all your arguments so far, Doctor, that must be the weakest. You want me to leave the Mymon Key here so it won't get homesick? You'll have to do better than *that*.'

The brushed steel casing of the Nanobomb was lit up red with the light from its counter:

00:45:00…
00:44:59…

00:44:58…

With every passing second, the room remained silent, but for the single, high-pitched beep. Then, from beyond its door, there came the sound of many footsteps.

The door suddenly shuddered with a tremendous bang, a rounded dent appearing in its surface. Another bang, and another dent, this one more pronounced than the last. With the third heavy bang the door flew in on its hinges, slamming back against the wall with a thunderous clang.

The humans stood in the corridor, three of them still holding on to the girder they had used as a battering ram. Django stepped past them and entered the bomb chamber, his flowing white robes dragging along the floor behind him.

He approached the bomb, his eyes growing wide with wonder, and he sighed with satisfaction, placing his hands on its shining steel shell. He closed his eyes, and began to laugh.

'We have it!' he said. 'We have the weapon of the Bad.'

He turned to face his men once more, pointing back towards the fixtures that held the bomb in place.

'Break it out,' he growled. 'We are taking this back to the city.'

They left the cargo hold and passed along a narrow

corridor that was tilted downwards, clinging to rusting pipes and decaying vines for balance. Tuco was muttering under his breath.

'I'm sorry, Tuco, old chap,' said Slipstream. 'You'll have to speak up. I can't hear you.'

'This is sacrilege,' hissed Tuco. 'We have desecrated the Tower of Gobo. You are *stealing* his treasure.'

'Oh, so it's *Gobo's* treasure, now, is it? First we have the Doctor telling me it belongs *here*, and now *you're* telling me it belongs to a cartoon clown. Well that's just *spiffing*, isn't it?'

Tuco wheeled around, holding the flaming torch to Slipstream's face.

'You will *pay* for this when Django finds out. Oh yes… Tuco will tell Django all about this, and Django will make you pay.'

Slipstream glowered at the human, his eyes growing wider with impatience. They moved on down the tunnel, coming eventually to the vast chamber of the control room, and the cage-like walkway above it.

'Ah!' said Slipstream. 'We're here again. Yes… I think I can remember the way from here.' He turned now to Tuco. 'Sorry, old chap… What was it you were saying, back there? In the tunnel? Something about telling Django about this and Django making me pay?'

'Yes,' said Tuco. 'Django *will* make you pay.'

'Hmm. Not sure about *that*.'

With that, Slipstream aimed his gun and fired. The blast slammed into Tuco, flinging him over the edge of the walkway. Seconds later, his body landed in the depths of the control room with a heavy thud.

The Doctor and Manco looked at one another and then Slipstream, both wide-eyed with shock.

'Yes,' said Slipstream, smiling malevolently. 'Seems we've come to the end of the road, chaps. You've rather outlived your purpose, I'm afraid. Very handy when we were navigating all those tunnels, but now…?'

'No, Slipstream,' said the Doctor. 'Don't do this. You've got the Mymon Key. You can just leave. I won't try and stop you.'

Slipstream laughed. 'You're a terrible liar, Doctor,' he said. 'We both know I could fly out of here and wherever I went you'd be waiting for me. No… Consider this my insurance policy.'

Slipstream aimed the gun at the Doctor's face, still grinning. He thumbed a green switch on the side of the blaster and it emitted a shrill squeal that rose in pitch.

'Now I'd like to say this will hurt me more than it'll hurt you, but it won't. It really won't. Goodbye, Doctor.'

His finger curled around the trigger, and he laughed with a brief derisive snort, but then he froze. His evaporating smile was replaced by a look of utter horror.

'Don't even think about it, Slipstream. Put the gun down.'

Standing behind him, with the barrel of his own gun touching the back of Slipstream's head, was Charlie, with Amy by his side.

'Damn and blast!' said Slipstream.

He spun around on his heels, ready to fire, but Charlie was quicker, and punched him full force in the face, breaking his nose. Slipstream staggered backwards, dropping his gun.

Acting quickly, the Doctor picked it up from the ground and hurled it out across the control room. The blaster tumbled through the air, spinning end over end. When it hit the ground it fired once, sending a bright green bolt of light ricocheting around the control room. Screens shattered and wall panels exploded, lighting up the vast room with cascading sparks. Then there was silence.

'Whoops,' said the Doctor. 'Should have thought that one through. Everyone OK? Manco? Amy?'

Manco nodded sheepishly, clearly dazed by everything that had happened in the last thirty seconds.

Amy simply beamed at him, and the Doctor smiled back.

Desperately, Slipstream scrambled to his feet, and was about to make a run for it when Charlie pinned him up against the railing, aiming the gun at him once more.

'I don't think so, somehow,' he said. 'Not this time. Give me one good reason why I shouldn't just shoot you. Right now.'

'Er… Hello?' said the Doctor, standing at Charlie's side. 'Remember me? We met earlier. Got off on the wrong foot, but I reckon we can put that behind us. Anyway… I think there's been enough death for one day. This man belongs behind bars. We're taking him with us.'

Still seething with anger, Charlie glowered at the Doctor. Then he looked at Amy, and the look she gave in return was clearly all it took to persuade him.

'OK,' he said. 'Come on, then. Let's go.'

They left the control room, and made their descent further down into the ship, along the last stretch of corridors that would take them out into the human city.

As they walked side by side, the Doctor turned to Amy.

'So…' he said. 'How are you? Miss me?'

Amy nodded enthusiastically, her eyes dewy with the promise of tears, and then she threw her arms around him with such force that it knocked the air out of his lungs.

The Doctor laughed and patted her back. 'I'll take that as a yes,' he said, then whispered in her ear: 'I'm so glad you're OK.'

They carried on walking.

'Well, *yeah*,' said Amy. 'I'm fine. And actually… Seems to me that *you* were the one who needed rescuing this time.'

'What's that supposed to mean?'

'Back there? You were in *quite* a lot of trouble. Until me and Charlie turned up, that is.'

'Oh really? Until you and Charlie turned up? So… You and Charlie, eh? Been making friends, have we?'

'And what's *that* supposed to mean? Are you *jealous*?'

'Jealous? Me? What? No! Jealous? I don't know what you're talking about.'

'So I'm not allowed to make friends with other aliens, is that it?'

'Don't be facetious.'

'Ha ha… You *are*. You're jealous. You're, like, *green* with envy.'

'I'm not even going to dignify that with a response.'

'Ha… The *jealous* Doctor. Oh, that is priceless.'

'I am *not* jealous.'

'You *so* are. What's your doctorate in, anyway? Got a PhD in *jealousy*, have you?'

'Be quiet.'

They had reached the ship's exit. Manco tapped a code into the door's control panel and the hatch opened up. Holding the others back with a gesture of his hand, he leaned out into the street.

'What do you see?' asked the Doctor. 'Is the coast clear?'

Manco shook his head.

'No. They're near the western gate. Lots of them. We can't go that way. We'll have to use the south gate. Follow me.'

Walking in single file, the five of them stepped out of the ship and into the streets of the human city, with Charlie and Slipstream trailing behind. Charlie alternated his aim between Slipstream and the far end of the street, where a crowd of humans were congregating at the gate, as if in anticipation.

'What are they waiting for?' he asked.

The Doctor pointed at the sky, and looking up Charlie saw the blazing orb of the comet. It looked now like a ferocious eye, its centre so bright as to appear almost black. Its edges were lost in a shimmering haze.

'They're waiting for *that*,' said the Doctor.

Chapter
17

The small lump of ice and rock entered the upper atmosphere of the Gyre with a cacophonous bang, its outer crust breaking away like a shower of sparks. As it plummeted towards the surface, it dragged behind it a quivering tail of fire and smoke, and it made a sound like the rumbling of heavy thunder.

Down and down it fell, piercing a hole through the muggy green clouds, travelling at hundreds of metres a second, before slamming into the salt plain with astonishing force.

Though the fragment was no bigger than an egg by the time it struck, it left a crater more than four metres across, and sent a rippling shockwave out across the plain, hissing through the salt crystals.

It had crashed into the humans' path, no more than a hundred metres ahead, and all of them cowered in its wake, diving to the ground and covering their heads as if expecting a second onslaught.

All of them except Django.

Next to his throne, strapped to the eight-legged carriage with lengths of rope, was the Sittuun bomb. He couldn't read the markings on its outer casing; they were written in the language of the Olden Ones, which only the heretic, Manco the Wordslinger, could understand. Nor did he really understand the digital display, and the numbers that changed with every passing second. He knew enough, however, to understand that these digits were counting down.

00:34:01…

00:34:00…

00:33:59…

'We move on!' Django yelled at his men, who were slowly beginning to gather themselves. 'We move on!'

The caravan of humans began moving again, their machines hissing and chugging away, the foot soldiers trudging through the salt.

Django didn't take his eyes off the bomb. To him, it wasn't *just* a bomb. The truth was, he had little understanding of what it actually did. The Sittuun had tried to explain, when they sent their emissaries to the human city, but he hadn't really listened. Their words meant little to him, and he had little time for them. They were liars and servants of the Bad, of this he was sure. Why else would they wish to destroy this world before Gobo's return?

Django thought about the Bad. He remembered, as a child, being taken to the Chamber of Stories by his father. There, he and the other children were made to sit and watch the silent images of the Olden Ones projected onto a great screen, while one of the city's elders would tell them what the story was about.

The Bad didn't always look the same. His face would often change, but he always wore the same clothes – a black hat with a wide brim – and he often had a moustache.

The Bad had haunted Django's childhood nightmares, and had plagued his waking thoughts. He had known, early on, that the Star with the Green Tail would return in his lifetime. The Elders had predicted it. They had taught him that with each visit the Star drew a little closer to their world, and that one day it would come to them. They had taught him that the star was Gobo, and that one day it would save them from the Bad.

Now that day had come. The Bad had sent his servants, the Sittuun and the one calling himself the Doctor, to ruin everything, but Django had thwarted them. He had their bomb, and he had the one person capable of disarming it.

Manco.

'Warning. Warning. Coordinate delta three nine is corrupted. Warning. Warning. Coordinate delta three nine is corrupted.'

The voice of the *Golden Bough*'s alarm remained unnervingly calm and impassive, speaking in a dull, pre-recorded monotone, though the ship itself was struggling to stay in the air. As good a pilot as he knew he was, and as hard as he tried, Captain Jamal simply couldn't make it fly in a straight line. Each time he set the coordinates to fly east, towards the human city, the ship would bank sharply to the left or right, as if it was being rebounded by a magnetic force.

To make matters worse, lumps of smouldering rock were raining from the sky.

One of the comet's fragments had clipped a tail fin, though not enough to compromise the ship. The Captain had been lucky. This time.

Speed was the thing, he had decided. He simply couldn't get enough velocity on his approach to punch through whatever force was affecting the ship's systems. He needed more of a run-up, but that would mean flying *away* from the city and even the Gyre itself.

After his fifth attempt had failed, he realised it was his only choice.

Of course, he didn't *have* to go to the human city at all. He could leave the Gyre, right there and then. He could steer away from the salt plains and the distant city, and set a course for his home world. The journey might take a month or two, but he'd be free of this place once and for all.

Except his son was down there, somewhere.

When he'd first sat at this ship's controls he'd felt what he thought might be fear for the first time in his life; but it wasn't a fear of the humans, or what they were capable of. It wasn't a fear for his personal safety. It was fear for his son. He had fought long and hard to get him a job in the IEA. He had fought for his son's place on the *Beagle XXI*'s mission to the Gyre. His son was only here, on this terrible, barren world, because of him.

He wasn't going home alone.

The Captain steered the ship away from the city one last time, so that now all he could see ahead was the dark blue sky and the twinkling of distant stars. He hit the boosters, and was pinned back in his seat by the sudden thrust of acceleration, and he watched the sky grow darker still as the *Golden Bough* left the Gyre's thin and almost imperceptible atmosphere.

When he was a hundred miles out, he turned the ship around in a long and graceful arc, and now the Gyre lay before him; a vast and jagged disc of gnarled grey metal, fused together over aeons. He saw it in its entirety, from edge to edge. He saw the light from the nearest stars glittering on its crooked metal mountains, and he saw the vast white void of the salt plains near the human city. Looking up, he saw the blazing inferno of Schuler-Khan, now perilously close to the Gyre; pieces of it falling away like drops of burning rain.

This was it. This was his chance.

Captain Jamal pushed the control column forward, and began his descent.

'Manco, old chap… I thought you were showing us the way *out* of here?' said Slipstream, his voice laced with disdain.

Charlie nudged him with the rifle. 'Hey… Do us all a favour and shut up,' he snapped.

'This *is* the way out,' said Manco, mindless of the bitter exchange between Charlie and Slipstream. 'It's the *only* way out.'

They were back inside one of the buildings in the human city, creeping along a low passage, the walls of which were fashioned from beaten panels bearing the logos of long-forgotten companies. Some of them were logos Amy recognised, brands that had existed in her time, back home. Seeing them like this – tarnished and faded – made her feel sad, though she couldn't quite fathom why.

Maybe it was the thought that all the effort that people put into their lives, all that time working hard to buy things, could be reduced to nothing more than junk. Or the fact that everything looked so *old*. No, not just old. Everything looked *ancient*. The adverts for sportswear and soft drinks that lined the passage looked as weathered, as ancient and otherworldly, as Egyptian hieroglyphs and Roman mosaics.

Eventually they left the passage and found themselves at the entrance to a large, almost church-like space, where dozens of humans sat before a large canvas sheet. At the back of the chamber an ancient projector clicked and whirred. Its single lens cast a prism of multicoloured light onto the sheet, on which two Wild West gunslingers stood at opposite ends of a dusty street lined with clapboard shop fronts and saloons. One wore a white cowboy hat, the other black. Their hands were poised above six shooters in leather holsters, and the man in black scrutinised his foe with narrow, vulpine eyes. Amy was sure she had seen the film somewhere before, maybe on TV on a rainy Sunday afternoon. Why were these humans, in the year 250,339 watching it?

Standing beside the sheet, holding a rusted length of pipe like a staff, was the Elder – a human in dark black robes, his long, matted grey beard reaching all the way down his chest. His voice echoed out over the otherwise silent chamber, and Amy, the Doctor and the others stopped in the narrow entrance and listened to him.

'And the Bad travelled to El Paso, where he met with Zasquez, son of Gobo. And he said to him, "Where have you taken mankind? I wish to destroy them, for I hate them all." And Zasquez said, "My father, Gobo, has taken mankind far away from this world, to a place called Earth, so that they may be safe…"'

Amy turned to the Doctor.

'What *is* this?' she whispered. 'Why are they watching *Westerns*?'

'My guess?' the Doctor replied. 'Somebody on the ship had a *big* collection of Westerns. They've developed an entire culture based around the scraps of what survived the crash. Old Westerns… a cartoon clown…'

'But surely this film's got nothing to do with Gobo?'

'No. It hasn't,' said the Doctor.

His face suddenly lit up with a smile.

'*You*… are a genius.'

Without another word, he walked out into the room, making no effort to conceal his presence. The bearded man in black robes stopped talking and looked at the Doctor, his mouth opening and closing but failing to form words. One by one the humans sitting before the screen turned around, and they looked at the Doctor with the same expressions of shock and confusion.

'Who... who are you?' asked the Elder.

'I'm the Doctor. And you, my friend, are talking rubbish. Eighteen-carat, unadulterated rubbish.'

The Doctor produced his sonic screwdriver from his pocket, and pointed it back across the room at the projector. Its tip burned with a glowing emerald light, and the image on the screen flickered and shuddered, freezing for a few seconds before starting again. Now they heard the character of the man in black, the Bad as they called him, speaking with his own husky voice.

'You know you can't win this, Shane. Whyn't ya just get on your horse and ride out of here while you still have the chance?'

Then the man in the white hat spoke.

'Not today, Ramirez. You killed my brother.'

The room erupted into excited chattering, and from the narrow entrance Amy watched on, confused. What *was* the Doctor playing at? They had to get out of this place, and quickly, and there he was fixing their projector. Was he mad?

'They speak!' cried one of the humans. 'I can hear them! The Olden Ones! They speak!'

As the Chamber of Stories descended into chaos, Dirk Slipstream began backing away from the small party who were still hiding in the passage, moving as silently as he could. He had made it no more than five paces when Charlie wheeled around and aimed his gun at him.

'Yeah... Nice try, Slipstream,' he growled. 'Now get back here.'

Slipstream cursed under his breath and joined them once more, and this time Charlie didn't take his eyes off him.

'OK!' shouted the Doctor, rushing to the front of the room. 'Right... Listen up. This story, the one you're watching. It's a *film*. If I remember rightly it's a film called *The 8:10 To El Paso*. It's got nothing to do with Gobo, nothing to do with the star with the green tail. It's a *Western*. See... That guy there? His name isn't Zasquez. It's Shane. *Zachary Velasquez* was the captain of a ship that crashed here thousands of years ago. He's *not in this film*. And *him*? He's not *the Bad*... His name is Ramirez. And they're both *actors*. But that star... the one that's in the sky right now... that star is *very* real. And when it comes here, when it hits this place, it will destroy *everything*. Now... I think I can help you. No... I *know* I can help you... But you have to follow me. We are leaving this city, and we're going to my ship. And then we're leaving this place. For good. There's no coming back.'

The room fell silent. The Doctor looked at them all, his expression one of hope and quiet desperation.

'Well... Are you with me?' he asked, but still there was silence.

The bearded man in the black robes stood before

him, glowering at the Doctor. 'Leave this place,' he said.

'I'm sorry…' said the Doctor. 'Didn't you hear what I just said?' He pointed at the screen. 'Didn't you hear what *they* said? They're *not* talking about Gobo. They're not talking about this place, or about the Olden Ones. It's just a *film*. You *have* to believe me. You are all in great danger.'

The Doctor looked to the audience, but none of them spoke. Not one of them even *moved*. Amy now knew what the Doctor was at least *trying* to do, but she also knew it was hopeless. She and the others stepped out from the tunnel and into the room, making their way gingerly towards the Doctor, as if they were treading across a minefield.

'Doctor,' she said. 'We *have* to go.'

The Doctor started shaking his head.

'No…' he said, still talking to the audience. 'You *have* to believe me. Please. I'm trying to *save* you.'

Manco placed one hand on the Doctor's shoulder.

'They never listen,' he said quietly. 'We must go now.'

'Come on,' said Charlie more forcefully. 'We haven't got *time*.'

He grabbed the Doctor roughly by the arm, pulling him out of the room, away from the screen and the silent audience, and the Doctor struggled in his grasp, still facing the humans.

'Please!' he shouted. 'If you stay here you are all going to *die*!'

He was still calling out to them when he was far away from that room and the humans, too far away for them to hear him.

Chapter
18

In the short time she had known him, Amy had never seen the Doctor like this. She had seen him angry, and thoughtful, and upset, but this was different. He hadn't spoken since they had reached the south gate of the city and made their way out onto the salt plain. He looked pale and drawn, and so much *older*, his boyish enthusiasm nowhere to be seen.

She could understand why. There had been children in the crowd watching the old film. Children who were now doomed, whichever way you looked at it. She had half expected the Doctor to come up with some last-minute solution, something which would solve everything, but the expression on his face told her that wasn't about to happen.

They were about a hundred metres away from the human city when Manco stopped walking. The Doctor turned around to face him.

'What's up?' he asked.

'I'm not coming,' said Manco. 'I'm staying here.'

The Doctor blinked twice and started shaking his head. 'No, Manco, listen... We can get you out of here. We can take you far away from here.'

'I know, Doctor. But I'm staying.'

'But *why*? You *know* what's about to happen.'

'Yes.'

'So come with us.'

'I can't. Where will you take me, Doctor? Earth? The *real* Earth? What would I do there? Would the humans there accept me? Would they treat me as their own? I doubt that. I'm like those... those *fish* that we saw... inside the tower. You said yourself, that's the only place where they exist. And the key... the one we found there. You said it *belonged* here, that there was no other place for it. Well that's me. There is no other place. We aren't like the humans on Earth, Doctor. We've been here too long.'

'But, Manco, *please*...'

'No, Doctor. I'm staying.'

Charlie moved to the Doctor's side. 'Come on... We *have* to go. If I know my Dad he'll have programmed the bomb by now. We don't have any time.'

The Doctor turned to Slipstream.

'The Key,' he said. 'You still have it.'

Slipstream huffed indignantly, reaching into his pocket and lifting out the polished, golden orb.

'Yes.'

'Give it to me.'

With another petulant huff, Slipstream handed the key to the Doctor, who in turn gave it to Manco.

'Take this with you,' he said. 'It belongs here.'

'Yes, Doctor,' said Manco, with a sad smile. 'And so do I.'

He nodded at each of them in turn, but said nothing more, and then he walked back towards the human city, still holding the Mymon Key in his hand.

'Let's go,' said Charlie. 'There's nothing you can do, Doctor.'

They walked on across the salt plain, with Amy at the Doctor's side. She looked up at him, trying to find the right words, but it was no use. What could she say that would make him feel better? Everything seemed so hopeless. The only thing she could do was reach out and hold his hand, and she was grateful, if just a little surprised, when he squeezed it in return and kept on holding it as they walked.

Charlie and Slipstream were in front, with Charlie's gun still trained on the prisoner.

'So,' drawled Slipstream, 'Do any of you *bright sparks* know how we're getting back to my ship? The bridge is out, and that swamp is infested with man-eating slugs. Any suggestions? Anybody?'

'We'll take *Bird*,' said Charlie.

'And what, pray tell, is *Bird*?'

'The helipod. I left it on the edge of the swamp.'

'But wait,' said Amy. 'There was barely enough room in that thing for *two* of us, let alone four.'

Slipstream laughed incredulously. 'Oh, well isn't that *marvellous*? Alien Boy's plan involves squeezing four fully grown adults in a flying shoebox. That's just *spiffing*.'

Charlie scowled at him. 'We could always leave you here,' he snapped. 'That would suit me right down to the ground.'

'Yes, I'm sure you'd like that, wouldn't you?'

The Doctor let go of Amy's hand, and he took several long strides so that he was now standing between Charlie and Slipstream.

'Play nice, children,' he said, then pointed at the sky. 'Look!'

The four of them had stopped walking and now, looking up, they saw something hurtling towards them. It started as just a tiny, yellow dot hovering above the horizon, but gradually it grew bigger, swaying from side to side and juddering violently.

'That's my bloody ship!' shouted Slipstream.

'Why of all the—'

'But who's flying it?' asked Amy. 'I mean… *You're* here. Charlie's here.'

'It's my Dad,' said Charlie, smiling. 'It has to be.'

Just then, as all four of them were about to breathe a collective sigh of relief, three chunks of comet came streaking out of the sky, screaming like fireworks. The *Golden Bough* swooped and dived between the missiles with the fleetness of an insect, dodging each of them, but now the fragments were bearing down towards the salt plain.

They slammed into the surface of the Gyre, only a few hundred metres away from where they stood, and there was but a second's pause before the deafening triple boom knocked them to the ground. They scrambled to their feet as quickly as they could, and started running.

The *Golden Bough* was getting closer now, still jerking about in the sky. It passed over the distant swamp, the tall plastic tubes swaying wildly in its wake, and it came out over the salt plain, its thrusters stirring up great clouds of powdered salt.

Amy tripped and fell as she ran, grazing her hands on the rough ground. She cried out in pain, but the Doctor lifted her to her feet with his arm around her waist, and he half carried her as they ran on, ever closer to where the *Golden Bough* now hovered over the salt plain, only a short distance away.

As they drew closer, they could see Captain Jamal at the ship's controls. He looked angry, or frustrated, and the ship lurched turbulently, as if it was bouncing on waves. Each time it lowered it would get to within a few feet of the surface before being launched back up into the air thirty metres or more.

They heard the Captain's voice, amplified by speakers in the ship's hull.

'It's no use!' he shouted. 'This thing won't land. The systems are all shot. It's this place... the Gyre...'

In the distance another fragment of the comet came crashing down with a thunderous boom, and the ground beneath them convulsed.

Everybody turned to the Doctor.

'Why's everyone looking at me?'

Amy's eyes grew wider and she hunched her shoulders.

'Er... Because you usually have all the answers?'

'Oh. Right. Yes. Charlie!'

Charlie nodded.

'The helipod... Where is it?'

Above them, the *Golden Bough* bucked and shuddered again, its thrusters howling and kicking up swirling tornadoes of dust. Charlie had to shout just to be heard above the noise.

'It's at the edge of the swamp!' he said, pointing into the distance. 'Over there!'

'Right!' the Doctor yelled in return. He looked up at the ship, and at Captain Jamal, gesturing wildly with his arms and pointing at the sky.

'What are you saying?' shouted Captain Jamal, his voice still booming from the speakers. 'I don't understand!'

'GO UP!' yelled the Doctor. 'GO! UP!'

Captain Jamal looked down at his son, and Charlie nodded. There was a moment's unspoken communication between them, when Amy saw just how deeply afraid they both were. And Charlie had told her the Sittuun had no fear...

With a terrific whoosh, the *Golden Bough* rose up into the dark sky, and the Doctor, Amy, Charlie and Slipstream carried on running across the salt plain, towards the swamp's edge. As they neared it, they saw countless Sollogs, their bodies liquefying into a greenish ooze, lying in the salt.

'What's happening to them?' Amy asked, still running.

'It's the comet,' the Doctor replied. 'They're running scared, and they don't care where they're running.'

'Kind of like us, then?' said Amy.

The Doctor smiled at her. 'Well, *I'm* not scared. You scared? I'm not scared.'

'Yeah, pull the other one.'

Twenty metres ahead of them, the ground burst open as yet another sliver of the comet slammed into the Gyre. Salt crystals and lumps of misshapen metal came raining down around them, but they didn't stop running.

'OK,' said the Doctor. 'Maybe just a *little* bit.'

They ran around the outer edge of the crater left by the last fragment, and Amy saw how it went down, deep below the surface of the salt plain, its centre filled with bubbling, molten metal. The thought that one of those things could hit any of them at any given moment, and that there was nothing they could do about it, filled her with terror, a terror that coursed through her veins and made her run even harder and faster than before.

She looked at the Doctor, and wondered if he really *did* feel fear. If he did, it didn't show in his face. He looked like he had done this, or something like this, a thousand times before. Based on her experiences with him so far, she'd say he probably had, and this made her feel very suddenly that little bit safer.

When they reached *Bird*, Charlie's helipod, Slipstream stopped running, struggling to catch his breath, and he braced himself on his knees.

'That thing?' he said. 'We're flying in that *contraption*?'

Charlie nodded.

'Are you *insane*, man? It's like a child's *toy*!'

'I know,' said Charlie. 'Two of us'll have to hold on to the outside.'

He looked from Slipstream to the Doctor and back again.

'Oh, I see,' said Slipstream. 'So I take it I'm one of the two, then?'

'Yes,' Charlie replied bluntly. 'You are.'

Without further hesitation, he opened up the helipod's hatch and climbed inside, inviting Amy to join him. Amy turned back to the Doctor.

'You should get in,' she said. 'Charlie can take us back to the TARDIS, but you're the only one who can fly it. You should be inside, where it's safer.'

The Doctor looked at her with an expression she couldn't quite read. He looked surprised, sad and deeply moved, all at the same time.

'No,' he said. 'No. You get in. I'll be fine. Trust me.'

Amy nodded and climbed into the helipod, and then Charlie closed the hatch behind them. Seconds later, the engines whirred into life, and the twin horizontal propellers behind the cabin began chopping at the air. The Doctor took up his position to one side of the craft, his feet balancing precariously on one of its runners, clinging by his fingertips to the cabin's roof. He looked at Slipstream. 'Are you coming?' he asked.

Slipstream looked back across the salt plain;

at the smouldering craters that pockmarked its glistening surface and at the fires that had broken out in the human city. He sighed and closed his eyes, then he climbed onto the helipod. The Doctor slapped his hand twice on the cabin roof, and they took off.

Inside the cabin, Amy and Charlie sat squeezed into a seat designed for one.

'OK. Where are we going?' asked Charlie.

'Take us to the TARDIS,' Amy replied. 'Remember? Back where you found us?'

Charlie nodded. He lifted a small receiver to his mouth, and twisted a dial on the dashboard.

'*Golden Bough, Golden Bough…*' he said. 'This is *Bird 1*. Are you receiving me? Over.'

There was a moment's near silence at the other end of the line, when all they could hear was the faint hiss of static, but then…

'Hearing you loud and clear, *Bird 1*.' It was the voice of Captain Jamal. 'What is your location? Over.'

'We're heading back to the copper valley, to the Doctor's ship. He can bring us to you. Over.'

'Copy that, *Bird 1*.'

Another pause, but Amy was sure she could hear the Captain breathing at the other end of the line.

'I'm so glad you're OK… Charlie,' he said at last, his voice now trembling with emotion.

'Copy that, Dad,' said Charlie. 'Over and out.'

They flew west, over the tangled black nest of plastic tubes and putrid green waters of the swamp. The helipod flew only a short distance above the tubes, the downdraft from its propellers striking a series of ghostly, atonal chords as they passed over them.

The Doctor rapped his knuckles against the window three times.

'What is it?' Amy asked.

The Doctor pointed skywards.

'Higher!' he mouthed. 'We need to go higher!'

Amy turned to Charlie. 'He says we need to go higher.'

'Well we *can't*,' Charlie replied. 'This thing isn't designed to carry this kind of weight.'

Thunk-thunk-thunk. The Doctor was knocking at the window again, and still peering in at them both.

'Higher!' he mouthed, pointing at the sky. 'Go! Higher!'

Amy shrugged helplessly, and then she heard a heavy thud, and the back end of the helipod seemed to dip back, as if burdened with yet another passenger.

'What was that?' she asked. 'Charlie... What *was* that?'

Charlie leaned to one side, trying to see what had happened in one of the helipod's mirrors.

'Not sure,' he replied. 'But it didn't sound good.'

Something was happening outside the cabin. The Doctor was balancing with one foot on the runner, and frantically kicking at something out of Amy's view. Slipstream, meanwhile, edged his way towards the front of the helipod's cabin, as if he was backing away from something. The Doctor pulled himself back, and now both he and Slipstream were nearing the nose of the helipod, both still facing backwards, wide-eyed and almost paralysed with fear.

There was a heavy but somehow soggy-sounding thump as something landed on the transparent ceiling of the cabin, and Amy looked up to see a single, suction-cup foot stuck to the glass.

'Oh no,' she said, and then again, 'Ohhh no.'

Another slimy foot came down and attached itself to the cabin roof. Then another. And another.

The Sollog crept its way out over the top of the helipod, so that it was almost blocking Charlie's view of the landscape ahead. Its eight feet hit the glass with a series of sickening plops as it drew closer to the Doctor and Slipstream.

'Please let it eat Slipstream… please let it eat Slipstream…' said Charlie, and Amy looked at him, shocked though not necessarily appalled.

'Do something!' she said.

'Like what?'

'I don't know. Try jiggling it up and down.'

'*Jiggling* it up and down? What does *jiggling* mean?'

'You know… *jiggling*. Go up and down. Try *shaking* it off.'

'Right. OK. Jiggling.'

Charlie gripped the helipod's control column and began shaking it vigorously. The whole craft shuddered in mid air, its nose tipping suddenly towards the ground and then jolting back up again. The Doctor and Slipstream both stumbled back, barely managing to hold on, and the Sollog staggered clumsily from side to side.

'Do it again!' Amy shouted.

Charlie nodded, and once again the helipod jolted up and down. This time the Sollog lost its footing altogether, and was sent skidding back across the roof, emitting a monstrous, high-pitched scream as it fell. There was a sickening splatter and crunch as it was sucked into one of the propellers, and a bright green gunk was sprayed out in all directions.

Hit full force by the shower of slime, the Doctor and Slipstream fell from sight.

'No!' Amy screamed, her hands pressed flat against the glass.

She couldn't see either of them. All that was visible, through the film of green slime now drizzling down the window, were the smouldering mounds of junk and the burning craters below them.

Then, with a heavy thump, a single hand came up and grasped the helipod's nose. It was followed, seconds later, by another, and then she saw the Doctor, pulling himself up. He was covered in what looked all too much like snot, and was far from amused. Bracing himself against the winds and the jolting movements of the helipod, the Doctor leaned around the nose of the craft. Reaching out with his hand and straining with all his strength, he lifted Slipstream up to safety.

'Did he *have* to do that?' said Charlie, shaking his head.

'Yes,' Amy replied, and then, as if it were self-explanatory, 'He's the Doctor.'

A red light started flashing on the dashboard, and a loud repeated buzzing sound filled the cabin.

'What's that?' asked Amy.

Charlie took in a deep breath and winced.

'We've lost engine one,' he said. 'We're going down.'

Chapter
19

The helipod clipped the razor-sharp ridge above the valley, and the jagged metal sliced through one of its runners like a hot knife through butter, narrowly missing the Doctor's foot.

For just a fraction of a second, the craft seemed to recover, rising up above the valley, its single working engine howling with the effort, but then it plummeted again. The runners met the ground with a terrific screech, showers of bright orange sparks erupting in their wake.

The Doctor looked at Slipstream across the nose of the helipod. Though only an hour or so earlier the man had tried to kill him, the Doctor took no pleasure in seeing him look quite this terrified.

'Hold on tight!' he shouted.

With its runners still squealing against the embankment of scrap metal, the helipod raced down the hillside like a toboggan, every slight bump causing it to shudder violently. Inside the cabin, Amy and Charlie were helpless at the controls. There was nothing they could do now but wait for the moment when they would reach the bottom.

That moment came a split second later, when the helipod came to a sudden, crashing halt. The Doctor and Slipstream were flung clear of the craft, tumbling end over end through the dust and the refuse.

Landing awkwardly on his back, the Doctor coughed and spluttered and groaned with pain before getting to his feet. The dust and debris were beginning to settle, and he saw the helipod resting nose-first in a mound of scrap. Its hatch creaked open, and Amy and Charlie climbed out, both still dazed by the impact.

'Where's Slipstream?' Amy asked, as she made her way toward the Doctor.

Scanning the bottom of the valley, the Doctor saw Slipstream lying face down and spread-eagled. He ran to his side, and turned him over. He was still breathing, but his eyes were closed.

'He's OK,' said the Doctor. 'Unconscious, but OK.'

'That's a shame,' said Charlie. 'Can't we just

leave him here?'

'No!' shouted the Doctor and Amy in unison.

'Joke! It was a joke! Well… kind of.'

Charlie shook his head. Leaning forward he lifted Slipstream from the ground with surprising strength and in one swift move hoisted him onto his shoulder.

'Right!' said the Doctor, clapping his hands and rubbing them together. 'The TARDIS!'

They ran through the valley, away from the upturned, buckled wreckage of the helipod. All they could hear now was the heavy, thunder-like boom of the comet's fragments slamming into the Gyre; a distant, monstrous drumbeat that rumbled and echoed through the night.

It crossed the Doctor's mind, for just one terrifying moment, that when they got to the TARDIS they would find it smashed into a million pieces at the bottom of a gaping crater. Nothing was certain any more. His mind was plagued with the image of the humans in their makeshift theatre, watching ancient films on a sagging canvas screen. He replayed that moment over and over again in his mind, trying to think of something else he could have said or done, something that would have convinced them to join him.

But then what would he have done? Would a hundred of them have made it across the swamp full of Sollogs? Would even two more have been able to cling to the helipod? As much as it pained him, he had to face the fact that there was little he could have done.

At least, he told himself, Amy was OK. More than OK, in fact. The little girl from Leadworth with the monster in her wall, the little girl who had waited so patiently for his return, was running across this terrifying alien landscape with a confidence that took him almost by surprise. If leaving the other humans here to meet their fate was a loss, then having Amy beside him took some of the pain out of losing.

And the TARDIS was exactly where they had left it, and in one piece.

When it first appeared around the corner, Amy turned to the Doctor, beaming, and he smiled back, and together they ran the rest of the journey, even faster than before. The Doctor stood before the TARDIS, placing his hands on its bright blue wooden exterior. He laughed with relief, and then he opened the door and ran inside, and Amy followed.

'Home again, home again!' said the Doctor, gazing up at the ceiling of the control room. 'Did you miss me? I missed *you*...'

'Er... you do know that you're talking to it?' said Amy, standing at his side.

'Oh yes. And she can hear every word.'

Behind them, Charlie was dragging Slipstream

through the open door. When he was only a little way in, he dropped him to the ground and gasped.

'It's... it's...'

Amy and the Doctor spoke as one: 'Bigger on the inside than it is on the outside?'

Charlie nodded, and the Doctor and Amy gave each other a 'high five'. The Doctor turned to Amy and frowned.

'I'm not sure about that.'

'About what?'

'The high five.'

'Are you not?'

'No. Are you?'

'Hmm. Not really, no.'

'Right. I just thought I'd try it out for size, but now... No. I'm not so sure.'

'OK. Well let's not do it again.'

'OK.'

'Right.' The Doctor turned to Charlie. 'Charlie... shut the door. Amy... see if you can wake up Sleeping Beauty over there. And let's get out of here.'

'Aye aye, captain,' said Charlie, offering a mock salute and slamming the door shut.

The Doctor rubbed his hands together and began operating the controls of the TARDIS, pressing buttons and pulling levers. The columns in its central console rose and fell, glowing with an otherworldly brilliance, and the room was filled with a metallic roar, the sound of time and space itself being folded as easily as a child might fold a piece of paper.

In the valley of ancient scrap metal, and in a blaze of white light and crackling bolts of electricity, the TARDIS vanished as quickly as it had appeared.

Seconds later, in an eruption of fire and debris, the valley itself was destroyed by another hurtling fragment from the comet Schuler-Khan.

Manco sat at the base of the tower which had once been the *Herald of Nanking*, and he looked up at the grinning, cartoon face of Gobo. He thought about the Doctor, and his friends, and even Slipstream, and he wondered if they had made it.

All around him, his people cowered before the tower on their hands and knees and begged Gobo to save them. He couldn't bring himself to tell them it was all a lie. They wouldn't listen and, besides, what comfort would that bring them? Better, he decided, to leave them clinging on to hope. After all, for all the knowledge he now had, what hope had it given him? As scared as those around him might be, he was the only one who understood how truly desperate the situation was.

He thought now about the three Sittuun who had come to their city, and told them about the 'comet'. He remembered how desperate they had sounded, when they explained their mission and what would happen if it failed. They had talked of a dozen neighbouring worlds, places the humans had never heard of. Billions of lives. It was a figure Manco had never even considered. Django had simply laughed at them before passing his sentence, condemning them to death.

And now Django was out there, somewhere, doing everything he could to stop the Sittuun, mindless of what would happen to all those other worlds, and all those other people.

Manco was lost in these thoughts when all around him the people began screaming. He looked around and saw them gazing up, still wailing, and pointing at yet another blazing fireball as it tore across the sky.

It smashed into the tower, straight into the colossal face of Gobo, punching a hole straight through the enormous metal structure and erupting from the other side in a great big ball of fire and tumbling debris. The image of Gobo was no more, a gaping, smouldering cavern all that was left. Shards of metal rained down into the city's streets. With an echoing metallic groan, the back end of the *Herald of Nanking* began to collapse, falling away from the rest of the structure and crashing down onto the city.

Its scale was so vast that it seemed to move quite slowly. It hit the ground with a deafening crunch, tons of metal caving in and disintegrating on impact, and a volcanic plume of dust was flung up into the air.

Manco could only look on in awe, while those around him ran screaming from the dust cloud.

'Are you Manco?'

The voice stirred him from his thoughts, and he saw one of Django's guards, sneering down at him. The air around them was choking up with dust and smoke. Manco nodded.

'You're coming with us,' said the guard, grabbing Manco by the arm and pulling him to his feet.

'But where are you taking me?' asked Manco.

'To Django.' The guard replied, with murderous intent.

First there was the noise: a harsh metallic grinding coming from somewhere deep inside the ship. Then a red light on the dashboard began to flash, and he heard the ship's voice, as nonchalant as ever.

'Warning. Warning. Foreign object located in loading bay. Warning. Warning. Foreign object located in loading bay.'

Activating the ship's automatic controls, Captain Jamal got up and ran from the cockpit down into the bowels of the *Golden Bough*. There, between stacked containers, he found a dark blue box with a white light flashing on its roof. The light stopped and the loading bay was silent once more.

Captain Jamal held his breath.

The door opened, and through it, for just one moment, the Captain was sure he could see what looked like a cavernous control room. But that was impossible. Wasn't it?

Then he saw his son.

Charlie stepped out of the blue box, looked at his father and smiled – an awkward grin, as if he wasn't sure what his father's reaction would be.

Captain Jamal ran to him, and threw his arms around him, and held him as tightly as he could.

'I thought I'd lost you,' he gasped. 'I thought I'd never see you again. What happened to Ahmed?'

'He didn't make it,' said Charlie, solemnly.

'What about Dr Heeva? Where is she?'

Captain Jamal shook his head.

'Oh, Dad… I'm so sorry.'

There were other people stepping out of the blue box now. First Amy, and then the stranger the Captain had seen with them on the salt plain, the Doctor, came out, pulling an unconscious Slipstream by his arms.

'Somebody give me a hand with this?' said the Doctor. 'For a skinny bloke he's quite heavy.'

Captain Jamal nodded, and helped the Doctor carry Slipstream to a corner of the loading bay, where they sat him up against one of the crates.

'What happened?' asked the Captain.

'Long story,' the Doctor told him. 'In a nutshell,

Slipstream here's a bit of a bad egg.'

'A *bit*?' said Amy. 'He tried to *kill* you.'

'Well, yes... But he didn't. Thanks to you and Charlie. Splendid work. Both of you. Now, Captain... We have to get out of here. Like... Now.'

Captain Jamal nodded urgently, and ran from the loading bay back to the cockpit with the Doctor following close behind. He took to the ship's controls, deactivated the automatic pilot, and hit the thrusters.

The *Golden Bough* tilted back, the view from its windows turning from the sprawling grey landscape of the Gyre to the vast canopy of space. The engines roared, the whole ship shuddering, but something was wrong.

'What is it?' asked the Doctor. 'What's happening?'

'I don't know!' said Captain Jamal. 'Something's pulling us back. We're moving *backwards*.'

'So put your foot down!'

'I'm trying that, Doctor, but it's no use. We're going to crash.'

Chapter
20

Slipstream was still out cold. Amy had tried shaking him gently to wake him, but it wasn't working. Even the jolting and shuddering of the ship had done nothing to bring him around.

Eventually, losing patience, Charlie stepped forward and slapped him hard across the face.

'Oh, that felt good,' he said.

Slipstream stirred.

'I swear... I was nowhere *near* the convent,' he mumbled drowsily. Then he opened his eyes suddenly and sat up straight. 'What? Where am I? What's happening?'

He looked around the loading bay, and at the TARDIS.

'We're *here*?' he said. 'We're on my ship? But

how did we—'

'The Doctor,' said Amy. 'He saved you. We could have left you back on the Gyre.'

Slipstream glowered at her and then rubbed his eyes with the palms of his hands. As he lifted himself up, clinging on to a crate for balance, they heard the sound of clanking footsteps, and the Doctor came running down from the cockpit.

'Slipstream!' he shouted.

'Oh, hello, Doctor. Seems I owe you a debt of gratitude, or some such nonsense.'

'The Mymon Key,' said the Doctor. 'Where is it?'

Slipstream frowned at him. 'I'm sorry, old chap. Have you lost your marbles? We left it on the Gyre. Don't you remember?'

'The *real* Mymon Key,' the Doctor snapped. 'You still have it. Where is it?'

Amy and Charlie looked at one another in shock, before turning back to Slipstream.

'What?' said Amy. 'But we... he... I mean... we saw it... and he gave it to Manco... What's happening?'

Slipstream closed his eyes and groaned. 'You know something, Doctor? You must be the most *infuriatingly* astute man I have ever had the displeasure to meet.'

'So you *do* have it?' said the Doctor.

'Well what if I *do*? I'd say it was small reward for

all I've had to endure in that *dreadful* place.'

'We're crashing, Slipstream. The Mymon Key is pulling us back to the Gyre. *That* is why we had to leave it there. We can't take it with us.'

Slipstream was backing away from them now, shaking his head.

'Oh, no... I'm not falling for that one. You just want to keep it for yourself, don't you? No... I don't think so, somehow.'

He had stepped back no further than three paces when he found himself staring down the barrel of Charlie's blaster.

'Give it to him,' said Charlie. 'Give it to him, or I'll redecorate this ship with bits of your head. How does *that* sound?'

Slipstream groaned, his whole body practically vibrating with anger. Begrudgingly he reached into his pocket and produced the shining, golden orb.

'You can't say my copy wasn't a spot-on replica, though,' he said, holding it in the palm of his hand. 'Six months in the prison workshop, that took me. Damn you, Doctor.'

The Doctor snatched the Mymon Key from Slipstream's grasp.

'Right,' he said. 'Only one thing for it. I'm going back to the Gyre.'

'What?' gasped Amy.

'I have to,' said the Doctor. 'If we just jettison it, there's no way of guaranteeing it'll go back to the Gyre. It could just hover in space, and then all this… the Gyre, the shipwrecks… would start all over again. I have to take it back myself. I have to finish this.'

'Are you mad?' said Charlie. 'The bomb detonates in less than fifteen minutes. You'll never make it.'

The Doctor looked at them, his drawn expression of quiet contemplation turning rapidly into a smile.

'Really?' he said. 'Just watch me.'

They dragged him, holding him by the arms, through the ruins of the city, past smouldering lumps of debris and the burnt-out shells of houses like rotten, hollow teeth. Some streets were impassable, choked up with thick black smoke, and every building engulfed in flames. Others were filled with people, many of them screaming helplessly at the sky as everything around them burned.

It was the end of the world.

Even Django's palace was no longer there. Most of it had been pulverised when the tower collapsed. At least a quarter of the city had been destroyed in an instant, and the fires were beginning to spread. Flickering orange tongues of flame, some of them hundreds of feet tall, arced up over the ramshackle dwellings, scorching everything in their path. Pieces of the shattered tower were still falling away from what was left of it. Manco watched as a panel perhaps fifteen metres across buckled from the heat of the flames, its rivets popping out of their fixtures like bullets, and then the panel came falling down, tumbling towards the streets and landing with a deafening clang.

They entered a dark tunnel that led into the heart of the city's oldest depths, passing through the Chamber of Stories on their way. The audience still sat before the screen, which was blank now, the projector having been smashed into pieces by the Elder, or perhaps one of his assistants.

'Be not afraid,' said the Elder, his stentorian voice booming out across the chamber. 'For the Star is almost with us. Gobo the Great, creator of us all, is coming…'

In the fleeting seconds before they dragged him on into another tunnel, Manco looked out at the congregation, and saw the expressions of fear and hope on their faces. It was almost a relief to be taken away from that place, so he wouldn't have to see them again.

'What is it? What's wrong?'

The TARDIS shook forcefully, and the Doctor struggled to stay upright, clinging onto the console with all his strength. The glowing columns rose and fell, but with jerking, unsteady movements and the familiar, ancient groan of its drive sounded choppy and distorted. Little wonder, the Doctor thought, that ships had crashed on the Gyre and been unable to leave. And it was all thanks to the Mymon Key.

When it finally came to a halt, things were far from still. The ground was shaking, and from beyond the TARDIS's doors he heard the *thump thump thump* of Schuler-Khan's fragments slamming into the Gyre, more frequently than before. There was now barely a second between each impact.

He ran from the console, opened the door, and stepped out onto the edge of the salt plain. What had once been a pristine lake of glistening white crystals was now a blackened landscape of burning craters, billowing pillars of smoke rising up into the sky; the clouds above were lit up orange by the flames.

And there, only a few metres from where he stood, was the swamp. There were fires there, too, and the corrugated plastic tubes were melting from the heat. Somewhere in amongst the inferno, the Doctor could hear the sound of screaming Sollogs.

The Doctor took the Mymon Key from his pocket, and he looked down at its gleaming, polished surface. Once, the Hexion Geldmongers had been a great species, their empire spanning whole galaxies. Now, their civilisation was no more than a footnote in history, and this tiny golden orb was all that remained of them; the last memento of an entire race.

All that power. There were so many things he could do with something as powerful as the Mymon Key. So many things he could put right. With an object that powerful he would be invincible. Nobody would dare challenge him. He could take the TARDIS through black holes, crossing into parallel dimensions without worry. As small and inanimate as it was, the Mymon Key was the key to the universe itself.

No. The Mymon Key was too powerful for anyone to own, even the Doctor. He had to place it somewhere beyond temptation.

He closed his eyes and held his breath, and then, in one swift move, he hurled it into the swamp.

'He's done *what*?'

Captain Jamal stood from the controls of the *Golden Bough*, pacing back and forth and shaking his head in disbelief.

'We have to wait for him,' said Amy. 'He's coming back.'

'Oh, you think so?' said the Captain. 'That world is being smashed into pieces by the comet. The Nanobomb detonates in ten minutes. He's insane. We can fly out of here *now*. The ship's working fine now that he's taken that... that *key*, or whatever it is, away.'

'Exactly. And that's why we have to wait for

him. It's only because of him that we *can* fly out of here.'

Captain Jamal looked from Amy to his son, who stood near the stairs leading down into the loading bay.

'Dad,' said Charlie. 'Please…'

Captain Jamal sighed. 'Very well,' he said. 'He's got eight minutes. If he isn't back by then we're leaving.'

Amy closed her eyes, breathing out slowly. 'Thank you.'

She about-turned, and made her way past Charlie, back down the stairs into the loading bay. There was no way she was leaving without the Doctor. Not now, not after all that had happened to them that day. She had waited a very long time for him to come back to her – fourteen years in all – and while his timekeeping might leave a lot to be desired, she was pretty sure he would not have left without her.

Their escape from the Gyre, and from this distant future, was so close she could practically taste it. No… She had made up her mind. She wasn't going without him, and so she would wait in the loading bay for the TARDIS to return.

When she got there she found it empty. She hadn't expected the TARDIS to be back so soon, but she *had* expected to see Slipstream. Where had he gone?

Tiptoeing silently across the room, she glanced behind each stack of containers, and was about to call for Charlie when she felt an arm around her throat, and the cold metal of a gun against the side of her head.

'You stupid people never learn,' Slipstream whispered in her ear. 'Never leave the prisoner unattended, and for pity's sake don't leave him in the place where he keeps all his *guns*.'

Before she could scream, he clasped his hand over her mouth, and began dragging her back across the loading bay. In the far corner, near the ship's rear, was a small circular hatch, and Slipstream pressed his foot down onto a lever at its side. The hatch opened with a hiss, and then with one violent shove he pushed Amy down through the porthole.

She landed with a thump in a tiny, cramped space, like the inside of a ball. There were two small chairs, and a panel of controls, along with a tiny circular window through which she saw the burning landscape of the Gyre far below. Slipstream jumped in after her, still brandishing his gun, and he quickly set about flicking switches. The lights on the miniature dashboard flickered into life, and the hatch door closed behind them with a bang.

'What are you *doing*?' Amy shouted.

'That Key was *mine*, damn it!' hissed Slipstream, still punching keys. 'Do you have *any* idea how long I've planned this? Do you? I'm not letting some time-travelling do-gooder and his silly little girlfriend ruin everything. Not today.'

'I'm not his *girlfriend*, actually,' snapped Amy, but then her voice was drowned out by the sound of a familiar and listless pre-recorded voice.

'Initiating escape sequence. Please authorise.'

Slipstream slammed his fist down on a bright red button, and all at once Amy felt her stomach lurch. Then they were falling, away from the hull of the *Golden Bough*, tumbling through the air, end over end, and hurtling back towards the surface of the Gyre.

Chapter
21

Shielding his eyes against the heat and the light of the flames, the Doctor watched as the Mymon Key sank down into the green waters of the swamp. In the last few seconds before it vanished, its polished gold surface shone out from the murky sludge, and then it was gone. Satisfied that it was done, that it was finished, the Doctor turned his back on the swamp and started running back towards the TARDIS.

He felt the ground beneath his feet tremble as, somewhere in the distance, another ball of rock hit the Gyre, but still he ran, and he was almost through the door and back inside the TARDIS when he saw something falling from the sky. For once, it was not a fragment of the comet but something small and man-made, and it descended towards the Gyre suspended from a parachute. As it got closer, the Doctor realised what it was.

It was an escape pod.

It only took another second or two for him to work out what that meant. There was only one person crazy – or greedy – enough to come back to this place.

The pod landed on the salt plain with a heavy thump, the parachute stretched out behind it on lengths of rope, bouncing and rippling in the wind. All around it the surface of the salt plain was being torn up by falling embers, their sudden, fast descent marked by a scream, like the sound of rockets being fired. Pieces of shrapnel, torn up from the Gyre's surface, were flying in all directions, making the Doctor's journey all the more perilous. As he ran towards the pod, he shielded his eyes against the flying shards of metal and rock, and the stinging spray of salt crystals. But still he ran.

The pod's hatch opened with a hiss, and he saw Amy climbing out. She landed a little awkwardly on her knees, and looked back over her shoulder as Slipstream clambered out after her, a blaster in his hand.

'Slipstream!' shouted the Doctor, struggling to be heard above the howling winds and the vociferous rumbling of the comet fragments as they fell. When Slipstream saw him, he smiled callously and grabbed Amy, his arm around her neck and the blaster pointed at her head.

'Don't try anything, Doctor,' he said. 'Just give me the key.'

'I'm afraid I can't do that, Slipstream.'

'Oh, really? Well that *is* a shame. Doesn't do my reputation much good… shooting young girls. Gives a chap an awful lot of bad press. Just give me the *key*, Doctor…'

'I can't. I don't have it.'

Slipstream seethed, his eyes bulging with agitation.

'Don't… have it?' he snarled. 'What do you mean, you *don't have it*?'

'I mean I don't have it,' said the Doctor, rolling up his sleeves and turned his pockets inside-out, one by one. The only thing he had to show was the sonic screwdriver. 'I've thrown it away. See?'

Slipstream rolled his eyes and gasped for air, his anger now reaching a level of hysteria. He pushed Amy away with a violent shove and aimed his gun at the Doctor.

'You did *what*?' he screamed.

'I threw it into the swamp.'

'Oh, well, wasn't that *grown-up* of you, Doctor? Poor little Time Lord can't have it, so no one else can.'

He was marching towards the Doctor, still brandishing the gun, but then he pushed the Doctor out of his way and carried on stomping towards the swamp.

'Slipstream… Don't!' the Doctor cried. 'Even if you *do* find it, what will you do then? You can't escape from this place with the Mymon Key.'

'I'll find a way!' Slipstream roared, without looking back. 'Dirk Slipstream *always* finds a way!'

Amy ran to the Doctor's side, pulling gently on his arm.

'Doctor… We have to stop him… Those *things* are in there.'

But Slipstream had already begun wading his way into the swamp, the green water rising up past his ankles and his knees, until he was waist-deep in it.

'Slipstream!' the Doctor cried, running towards the swamp's edge. 'Come back! You'll never make it!'

'Won't I, Doctor?' yelled Slipstream, pushing aside the tightly packed plastic tubes, moving further and further away from them. 'Just watch me!'

He had disappeared now, lost in the forest of melting black plastic, and then the Doctor and Amy heard a familiar screech: the sound of the Sollogs. The swamp was lit up with the flare of Slipstream's blaster, and the sound of each shot rang out, for a moment drowning out even the noise of the Gyre's destruction. From somewhere deep inside the swamp, Slipstream screamed, still firing his gun, and then the gunshots and the screaming came to an abrupt end.

The Doctor looked away, his eyes closed. He put his arm around Amy's shoulder.

'Come on,' he said. 'Let's go.'

They ran across the salt plain to the TARDIS, neither of them speaking. The Doctor slammed the door behind them before leaping across the room to the console. Even with the doors shut, they could still hear the Gyre being smashed apart in its final, calamitous moments.

The glowing column began to rise and fall, and the room was filled with the sound of its metallic yawn, intertwined with a single, shrill tone that rose in pitch. The Doctor looked at Amy across the console and saw her expression of relief. There were no words that could properly express how glad he was to have her safe, and that they'd both got away from the Gyre in one piece. All he could do was smile at her, and Amy smiled back.

The sounds of the TARDIS died down, and they stepped out through its narrow door into the loading bay of the *Golden Bough*.

'You know, that still freaks me out a little bit,' said Amy.

'What does?'

'Well… The doors close and you're in one place. And then you open them again, and you're somewhere completely different.'

'A bit like an elevator, then?'

'No. It's nothing *like* an elevator. I mean, at least with an elevator you're in the same place, you're just on a different floor. With this… You're on a different planet. Or in a different *year*.'

'Yes. Well… that's kind of what the TARDIS does.'

'I *know* that… But it's still *weird*.'

They left the loading bay and climbed up its staircase to the cockpit, where Captain Jamal and Charlie were waiting for them. When he saw Amy, Charlie beamed and let out a long sigh of relief.

'You're OK!' he said.

Amy nodded.

'And Slipstream?'

The Doctor shook his head.

'Good work, Doctor,' said Captain Jamal, and then, a little sarcastically. 'So do I have your permission to get us out of here?'

'Yes you do,' said the Doctor. 'You really do.'

'Ah, Wordslinger…' Django purred as his guards dragged Manco into the dungeon.

With the palace destroyed, Manco had been taken deep under the city, back to the dungeon where, until only a few hours ago, he had been a prisoner. It felt strangely appropriate that it should end there.

Django was sitting on his throne next to the Sittuun's bomb.

Manco glared at his leader with resentment and anger, but he bit his lip and remained silent.

'Do you know what this is?' asked Django, placing one bony, almost skeletal hand on the bomb's outer casing.

Manco nodded. 'It's the bomb,' he said quietly.

'That's right,' said Django. 'It is the bomb. It is the work of the Bad. There are words on the bomb, Manco. Words written in the language of the Olden Ones. Instructions.'

Manco looked down to where Django was stroking the bomb, as if it were some kind of pet. He saw the words 'DEACTIVATION PROCEDURE' written in blood-red print, and next to those words a small clock, on which he saw the numbers counting down.

00:01:20…

00:01:19…

00:01:18…

'You must disarm the bomb, Manco. Disarm the bomb and we shall all be saved from this world. Gobo is coming.'

Manco shook his head. 'It's not true,' he said. 'None of it is true. If we deactivate that bomb the star… the Star with the Green Tail… it'll hit our world, and destroy so many others.'

Django's eyes grew wide and his lips curled

back from his greying, jagged teeth.

'There are no other worlds!' he roared. 'There is only the Earth, the creation of Gobo!'

'That's not true,' said Manco, softly. 'The man, the *Doctor*… He told me so. He told me I was *right*. We aren't from *here*, Django. We never were.'

'I have no time for this heresy. Disarm the bomb, Manco.'

One of the guards now stood at Manco's side, a sword against his throat, but Manco shook his head.

'No,' he said. 'Because I saw what the Doctor tried to do. He tried to save us. He stood there, in the Chamber of Stories, and he told people the truth, but they wouldn't *listen*. He is a *good* man, better than any of us, and it broke his heart. There were children in that room, Django. *Our* children. And your words, and your *lies*… You've condemned them all to death. No more should have to die because of us, because of what we've become, what you and those before you turned us into. It ends here and now, Django. You can threaten me with weapons all you like. I'm unarmed. I'm not a warrior… I'm the Wordslinger. My only weapon is a word, and that word is "No".'

Django rose up from his throne; his eyes bulging with impotent rage, the tendons and veins in his scrawny neck sticking out like the grooves in an ancient tree trunk, and spittle foaming in the corners of his mouth.

'I command you to disarm the bomb!' he howled.

Manco laughed.

'And what are you going to do, Django? Kill me? You can't hurt me any more than you already have. We're dead already, and we have been for a very long time.'

Manco looked once more to the bomb, and the numbers counting down on its display.

00:00:04...

00:00:03...

Django let out a terrifying, angry roar, and leapt towards Manco with his arms flailing wildly, but Manco just closed his eyes and smiled.

00:00:02...

00:00:01...

She had expected a noise; a tremendous bang that would deafen her and shake every bone in her body, but there was nothing. There wasn't even a flash of light, or a mushroom cloud, or anything else Amy might have expected from a bomb.

The explosion, if it could be called that, was silenced by their distance, and by the vacuum of space, and instead of a flash or an inferno all she saw was a darkness; a great gaping darkness that opened up like an aperture in the heart of the Gyre. In only a few seconds this darkness spread its way out across the bleak, metallic landscape, devouring everything in its wake. Mountain ranges disappeared in the time it took her to blink. The salt plains, the canyon, the desert of glass, all vanished in a fraction of a second.

As the Gyre evaporated before their eyes, all that was left, barely visible against the infinite black canvas of space, was a vague haze, as translucent as a fine mist. The comet, Schuler-Khan, travelling at fifty kilometres a second, punched through the haze, causing it to swirl and spiral in its wake, but nothing more.

Captain Jamal and Charlie let out a triumphant cheer, the Captain patting his son on the back, and putting his arm around his shoulder.

'We did it, Charlie,' he said. 'We actually did it.'

The Doctor was quiet. He had taken the co-pilot's seat but hadn't watched the Gyre's destruction with the others. It made Amy feel almost guilty for watching it herself. After all, it wasn't a firework display. They had just watched a whole world being destroyed.

As she looked at the Time Lord, her expression crumpled into a sympathetic frown, and she placed her hand on his shoulder.

'Hey… are you OK?' she asked.

The Doctor looked up at her, as if snapping out of a daydream.

'What's that?'

'I said, "Are you OK?"'

He thought about this for a moment, his eyebrows bunching together, and then he looked at her again.

'Are *you* OK?' he asked.

'Yeah. I'm OK,' replied Amy.

'Then yes… I'm OK.'

Chapter
22

The Doctor looked out from the windows of the *Golden Bough* at nothing but the twinkling stars, the nearest sun, and a handful of shining planets, all of them millions of miles away. With the destruction of the Gyre not one, but two civilisations had been erased from the pages of history, for ever. The descendants of the *Herald of Nanking*'s crew, who had survived for hundreds of thousands of years on that remote and barren world, were gone, as was the Mymon Key. Soon enough they would all be forgotten and never spoken of or thought about again. This was the rhythm of the universe, as predictable as a metronome. Civilisations, great and small, come and go; some are remembered for a while, but all of them forgotten in time.

The Doctor was joined eventually by Captain Jamal, who stepped into the cockpit and took to the pilot's seat.

'Well, Doctor… I don't think I can even *begin* to tell you how grateful I am.'

The Doctor frowned at him. 'Really?' he said. 'Why?'

'Well… Everything you did back there. We'd never have made it without you.'

The Doctor sighed. 'Do you think so?' he said. 'You should be thanking your son. He got me out of quite a scrape back there. And *he* was the one who flew us back to the TARDIS. I can't say I did a great deal, to tell you the truth.'

'Nonsense,' said the Captain, smiling softly. 'Neither Charlie nor I had even *heard* of the Mymon Key. Without you it would have stayed on the ship, with Slipstream, and we would have crashed. I lost enough crew on this mission. I couldn't bear losing my son too.'

The Doctor nodded, but his expression was still morose. Captain Jamal scrutinised him, as if trying to read his thoughts.

'You're thinking about the humans, aren't you?' he asked.

'Yes,' replied the Doctor. 'There were so many of them. And there was *nothing* I could do.'

The Captain nodded sympathetically and sighed.

'While we were on the Gyre,' he said, 'I told myself the humans were just savages. They certainly *acted* like savages. Most of them, anyway. And I told myself they were savages because it made my job easier. When they turned down our offer of help I knew that there were only two ways it could end. We could detonate the bomb and destroy the Gyre, or the Gyre would be hit by a comet, and pieces of it would be flung out across this entire system.'

He pointed out through the window, at one of the distant, shining planets: a tiny speck in the distance which looked a pale shade of blue.

'See that planet? That's our home world. There are a billion Sittuun there. My family, my friends... they are all there. Everything and everyone I've ever known. Our projections showed a *ninety eight per cent* chance of it being hit, should Schuler-Khan impact with the Gyre. The loss of life would have been *catastrophic*. But even with that in mind, and even after I'd learned to think of the humans as savages, I couldn't bring myself to do it. I sat there, with the bomb, but I couldn't set it. Tell me something, Doctor... We saw a signal, in Morse code, from the human city. Was that you?'

The Doctor nodded.

'I thought so,' said Captain Jamal, smiling. 'Well that signal probably saved our lives. Most of our lives, anyway. You know something, Doctor? For one who looks so young, you have an air about you. Like a man who's seen the universe several times over. I can't quite describe it. You've done this sort of thing before?'

'Yes. I suppose so.'

'And do things always go to plan?'

'Sometimes. Not always.'

'And this time?'

The Doctor shrugged and shook his head.

'Then I'd suggest, Doctor, that you think about it this way. Today you saved three lives several times over. Because of your warning, the bomb was activated and the Gyre destroyed. One world has been destroyed, but another *twelve* in this system are safe. The most important choices that we make in life are never the easiest. You're a good man, Doctor, and you did everything you could. We all did.'

'So I suppose you'll be going soon?' said Charlie.

He and Amy were in the loading bay, sat on crates either side of the TARDIS. Amy hadn't spoken in some time, and the silence was beginning to feel awkward.

'Yeah,' she replied. 'Soon.'

'Right. And this thing really *can* travel in time?'

Amy nodded.

'So you could go *anywhere*?'

'Yeah. Just about. Although I'll have to go home sooner or later. I can't keep putting *that* off.

I've got *such* a big day tomorrow. If you can call it tomorrow. I mean… It's not *really* tomorrow. It's a day two hundred and fifty thousand *years* ago. And between you and me, I'm having such a hard time getting my head around this stuff. It's like jetlag. But really, really *bad* jetlag. Like, when you get jetlag your body thinks it's nine o'clock in the morning, but it's three o'clock and everyone else is still asleep. Right now my brain thinks it's the twenty-first century. I've run around a spaceship in my *nightie*. How weird is that?'

Charlie laughed. 'Yeah. That *is* kind of weird. So… Have you got anyone back home?'

'What do you mean?'

'Well… Like, a boyfriend or anything?'

'It's a bit more complicated than that,' she told him, chewing her lip anxiously.

'Oh. I see. Only… You know, if you and the Doctor were planning on hanging around for a little while, maybe coming back to our planet for a bit, I thought, maybe…'

'Were you about to ask me out on a *date*?'

Charlie looked down at the ground, his cheeks turning a funny shade of turquoise. He could feel himself blushing, but was unable to stop it.

'Oh my God! You were!' said Amy. 'You were asking me out on a *date*! But… you're an *alien*!'

'Er… so are *you*,' said Charlie. 'From my perspective, I mean. I'm sorry. Forget I said anything. I understand. It's the *no-nose* thing, isn't it? Lots of Earth girls freak out with the *no-nose* thing. And that's fine. To be honest, I find eyebrows a little bit weird. I mean… It looks like your eyes are wearing tiny little wigs or something.'

Amy started to laugh and couldn't stop. She laughed until there were tears rolling down her cheeks, doubled over and hugging herself and almost falling from the crate. Charlie felt himself blushing again.

'What?' said Charlie. 'Well they *do*. I'm *sorry*.'

'Tiny little wigs…' Amy laughed. 'That's… that's hilarious.'

She wiped the tears from her eyes and took a deep breath, trying her best to compose herself.

'Oh, this is still so weird. I haven't laughed that hard in quite a while. I wasn't sure I still could… after that place.'

And now the smile faded from her face, and she looked thoughtful and pensive once more.

'I just keep thinking about the people who were there,' she said. 'I mean… I'm a human, and they were humans, but they seemed so different, when we first saw them. And then I started noticing things, when we were in their city. Familiar things. The things they were saying and doing. And I thought, hang on… they're not that different. They're not that different at all. I mean… All the wars and things that happen back on Earth. All the violence. How are we any better? And is that all we're really good at, at the end of the day? Just being horrible to each other? Certainly seems like it sometimes.'

Suddenly, Amy looked very sad and troubled, but Charlie knew exactly what to do. He got up from the crate, and crossed the loading bay to the far corner, where the Sittuun's possessions and supplies were stacked. He opened up what looked like a silver briefcase and took out a small white plastic cube. Placing the cube on top of the crate next to Amy's, he hit a button, and seconds later the loading bay was filled with the sound of an old, 1940s big band and then a woman's voice, singing: *'Let's build a stairway to the stars…'*

'What's *that*?' asked Amy, scrunching up her nose.

'*That…*' said Charlie, 'is Ella Fitzgerald. And she was human. Brilliant, isn't it?'

'Well… It's not really *my* kind of music. It's like the kind of thing somebody's *grandmother* would listen to. But… yeah… I suppose it's all right.'

'All right? All right? It's *beautiful*. We don't have anything like this back home. We don't have songs. We don't even have *music*. When I think about humans, Amy… I don't think about wars or anything like that. I think about *this*. This is what you lot are capable of. This and so much more. And it's *beautiful*.'

Amy laughed softly.

'I guess,' she said. 'You're not going to ask me to *dance*, are you?'

Charlie shook his head and smiled. 'No,' he said. 'Sittuun don't dance.'

Just then they heard the clanking sound of footsteps on the stairs and a familiar voice, singing along: '*The moon will guide us / As we go drifting along…*' The Doctor stepped down into the loading bay.

'Ella Fitzgerald!' he said. 'You know, I once jammed with her at the Roseland Ballroom. I played recorder. Didn't go down too well with the audience. Or her, for that matter. Anyway… Are you ready?'

Amy nodded. 'As I'll ever be.'

'Very well,' said the Doctor. 'In that case… to the TARDIS!'

He pointed at the little blue box with a dramatic flourish and then frowned.

'Was that a bit much?'

'Yeah,' said Amy. 'It was a bit. Don't do it again.'

'Right. OK. Funnily enough, it didn't feel the right last time I tried it.' He turned to Charlie. 'Goodbye, Charlie.'

'Goodbye, Doctor.'

With a sad, crumpled smile, Charlie looked at Amy.

'Bye, then,' he said.

'Yeah,' said Amy. 'Bye.'

And then she reached up and gave him a single kiss on the cheek. With his face once again turning an embarrassed shade of turquoise, Charlie laughed nervously, and gave a small bashful wave as the Doctor and Amy stepped into the TARDIS and closed the door behind them.

Moments later the light on its roof began to flash and the loading bay was filled with that noise, like the sound Charlie imagined a galaxy might make as it turns. First the TARDIS became translucent, the wall behind it appearing as a faint outline, and then the blue box and its two passengers were gone, leaving Charlie alone with the music.

BEAGLE XXI/OBJECT 556C INTERNAL INQUIRY
Final Conclusions

Though a thorough cross-system investigation found no records of 'the Doctor' (presumed human) or 'Amy Pond' (presumed human), both Captain Jamal al-Jehedeh and Lt Baasim 'Charlie' al-Jehedeh testify that, without their assistance, escape from Object 556/C would have been impossible, and the mission would have failed.

It is the decision of this board that all information regarding the human inhabitants of Object 556/C and the final fate of the *Herald of Nanking* should remain classified, in the interest of Human-Sittuun relations. The death of the wanted criminal Dirk Slipstream has been reported to both the Volag-Noc facility in Mutter's Spiral and the Intergalactic Crime Bureau.

It is this board's recommendation that all crew members of the *Beagle XXI*, surviving and deceased, are awarded the highest commendation the IEA can offer for their bravery and commitment: the Silver Helix. We would also recommend that Cpt. Jamal al-Jehedeh and Lt Baasim 'Charlie' al-Jehedeh are promoted forthwith, to the ranks of Admiral and Lieutenant Commander respectively.

'The Doctor' and 'Amy Pond' are awarded the Civilian Cross in absentia.

File status: Closed.

Acknowledgements

Big thanks to everyone at BBC Wales and BBC Books who helped along the way, including Gary Russell, Justin Richards, Steve Tribe and Edward Russell. Special thanks also to Lord Tinlegs (aka EF), who listened to the story in instalments, and to the writers and other animals with whom I discussed ideas, including Joe Lidster, Scott Handcock and Oli Smith. Lastly, a posthumous thankyou to Vaughan Williams's *Sinfonia Antartica*, which became the soundtrack to this book as I was writing it. If you've not heard it, I believe it is readily available on LP and cassette.

DOCTOR █ WHO
Apollo 23
by Justin Richards

£6.99 ISBN 978 1 846 07200 0

An astronaut in full spacesuit appears out of thin air in a busy shopping centre. Maybe it's a publicity stunt.

A photo shows a well-dressed woman in a red coat lying dead at the edge of a crater on the dark side of the moon, beside her beloved dog 'Poochie'. Maybe it's a hoax.

But as the Doctor and Amy find out, these are just minor events in a sinister plan to take over every human being on Earth. The plot centres on a secret military base on the moon – that's where Amy and the TARDIS are.

The Doctor is back on Earth, and without the TARDIS there's no way he can get to the moon to save Amy and defeat the aliens.

Or is there? The Doctor discovers one last great secret that could save humanity: Apollo 23.

A thrilling, all-new adventure featuring the Doctor and Amy, as played by Matt Smith and Karen Gillan in the spectacular hit series from BBC Television.

Coming soon from BBC Books:

DOCTOR ⬛ WHO
The TARDIS Handbook

by Steve Tribe

£12.99 ISBN 978 1 846 07986 3

The inside scoop on 900 years of travel aboard the Doctor's famous time machine.

Everything you need to know about the TARDIS is here – where it came from, where it's been, how it works, and how it has changed since we first encountered it in that East London junkyard in 1963.

Including photographs, design drawings and concept artwork from different eras of the series, this handbook explores the ship's endless interior, looking inside its wardrobe and bedrooms, its power rooms and sick bay, its corridors and cloisters, and revealing just how the show's production teams have created the dimensionally transcendental police box, inside and out.

The TARDIS Handbook is the essential guide to the best ship in the universe.

DOCTOR ⬚ WHO
The Glamour Chase

by Gary Russell

£6.99 ISBN 978 1 846 07988 7

An archaeological dig in 1936 unearths relics of another time... And – as the Doctor and Amy realise – another place. Another planet. But if Enola Porter, noted adventuress, has really found evidence of an alien civilisation, how come she isn't famous? How come Amy's never heard of her? Come to that, since she's been travelling with him for a while now, how come Amy's never even heard of the Doctor?

As the ancient spaceship reactivates, the Doctor discovers that nothing and no one can be trusted. The things that seem most real could actually be illusion. Obvious illusions could be real – and deadly.

Who can the Doctor trust when no one is what they seem? And how can he defeat an enemy who can bend reality itself to their will? For the Doctor and Amy – and all of humanity – the buried secrets of the past are very much a threat to the present...

A thrilling, all-new adventure featuring the Doctor and Amy, as played by Matt Smith and Karen Gillan in the spectacular hit series from BBC Television.

Coming soon from BBC Books:

DOCTOR WHO
Nuclear Time
by Oli Smith

£6.99 ISBN 978 1 846 07989 4

Colorado, 1981. The Doctor and Amy arrive in Appletown – an idyllic village in the remote American desert where the townsfolk go peacefully about their suburban routines. But when two more strangers arrive, things begin to change. The first is a mad scientist – whose warnings are cut short by an untimely and brutal death. The second is the Doctor…

As death falls from the sky, the Doctor is trapped. The TARDIS is damaged, and the Doctor finds he is living backwards through time. With Amy being hunted through the suburban streets of the Doctor's own future and getting farther away with every passing second, he must unravel the secrets of Appletown before time runs out…

A thrilling, all-new adventure featuring the Doctor and Amy, as played by Matt Smith and Karen Gillan in the spectacular hit series from BBC Television.